B Mc
D W

WES
BKM
new

Large Print Nye
Nye, Nelson C. 1907-
Come a-smokin'

WITHDRAWN

GAYLORD M

Also by Nelson Nye
in Large Print:

Desert of the Damned
Gun-Hunt for the Sundance Kid
The Last Bullet
The Texas Gun

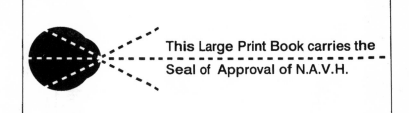

Come A-Smokin'

Nelson Nye

Thorndike Press • Waterville, Maine

Published in 2002 by arrangement with
Golden West Literary Agency.

Thorndike Press Large Print Paperback Series.

The tree indicium is a trademark of Thorndike Press.

The text of this Large Print edition is unabridged.
Other aspects of the book may vary from the original edition.

Set in 16 pt. Plantin by Rick Gundberg.

Printed in the United States on permanent paper.

Library of Congress Cataloging-in-Publication Data

Nye, Nelson C. (Nelson Coral), 1907-
   Come a-smokin' / Nelson Nye.
      p. cm.
   ISBN 0-7862-4457-7 (lg. print : sc : alk. paper)
   1. Impostors and imposture — Fiction. 2. Arizona —
Fiction. 3. Large type books. I. Title.
   PS3527.Y33 C65 2002
   813'.54—dc21   2002020382

FOR RUTH

WHO DEVISED MOST OF IT

Chapter 1

He was tall, whip lean and freckled with dust-streaked sunburnt features whose expression of drugged indifference masked a turmoil as explosive and deadly as the crust that covers a slumbering volcano. The last bite of stolen food had gone through his stomach three days ago and, though stolen money clanked in the pockets of the bedraggled stolen clothes he wore, the stolen freedom which had kept him going had been reckoned too precious to be risked through contact with the cupidity motivating others of his kind.

He cursed through cracked and beard stubbled lips as he peered from the fronds of a scraggly mesquite at a huddle of houses racked against the far slope. He had no idea what town this was or how near it might be to the Mexican border; only the encroaching proximity of starvation had pressured him into considering it at all. But he had reached the point where forced realization warned he hadn't much choice if he would continue to live.

He was two weeks out of Yuma; roughly a hundred and eighty miles east of it and God only knew how many miles south. He was still afoot, had no papers or weapons, and his name was Grete Marratt — which probably wouldn't mean much without you'd been concerned or had followed the trial in the Prescott, Phoenix or Tucson papers. In that case, unless you were connected with law enforcement or preferred to make your living from what you could catch in bounties, you'd be a heap inclined to give him all the room he wanted. According to the records Grete Marratt was a killer.

He had certainly rubbed out one man. Deliberately, coldbloodedly and with obvious malice aforethought, he had gunned him down on the main street of Prescott. The prosecution had produced thirty-seven independent witnesses. There had never been the slightest doubt about the outcome; but as a case it had caused an inordinate amount of jaw wagging because the fellow Marratt killed had been a Deputy U.S. Marshal.

Hugh Clagg, the deceased, had been a stranger in that section whereas Marratt had been well known, a rancher who had lived his entire thirty-two years in the region adjacent to Prescott. He'd been generally respected and had never been in serious trouble.

Clagg had been sent to look into a payroll stage robbery in which two sacks of mail had been taken. Subsequent investigation had thoroughly disproved any possibility of Marratt's having been involved in the case Clagg was working on. No connection had been found between the marshal and Marratt; so far as could be learned they had never exchanged two words up to the time of the shooting. Marratt had said something then but had spoken so guardedly no one else could repeat the few words he had used.

He wouldn't talk when arrested. What he felt, what he thought, was locked away secure behind a poker-face stare. "Think whatever you want — I've got nothing to say." He had stuck to that attitude all during the trial. Not even his friends could get any more out of him. And now, once again, he was on the loose; an escaped convict for whom men were watching the whole length of the border.

Another man might have laughed, at least been grimly amused at the concept of all those alerted tin-packers hunkered back of cocked rifles along a line he hadn't any intention of crossing.

Marratt never gave the matter a thought. He was far too engrossed with this business of survival, with staying alive till he could track down Clagg's partner, the three-fingered man with the uptilted nose and the jagged knife scar across his left temple. These were the things which were important to Marratt; these, with his need to stay out of the law's hands until this business was done with.

He was not a patient man but he could exercise patience. He had no flair for getting a gun out of leather but, once he had one focused, he could call his shots. The sight of blood turned his stomach but he had worlds of determination; it had survived five years of Yuma and would continue unabated until Clagg's partner joined the marshal.

Bella Loma wasn't much of a place, Marratt saw, even for Arizona. No more than the proverbial jog in the road, it contained four saloons, a big general store, a blacksmith shop, an assayer's office, a public corral with feed lot attached, three rooming houses, a crib, no homes and a packing-crate post office which, according to the sign crudely chalked on its door, was only open for business on Saturday nights. There was also a restaurant, if you cared to flatter the Lone Star Grub with the title.

It was lamp-lighting time when Marratt limped into the place and sagged onto a stool at the fly-blown counter. A blowsy, redfaced blonde with a once-white apron stretched across buxom breasts took his order and foghorned it over to the sallow-cheeked oldster bent above the greasy stove. There were half a dozen customers mingling conversation with the clatter of pans and dishes and though he propped both elbows on the oilcloth, hands cupping his face to mask all he could of his profile, Marratt kept his ears skinned for any mention of his name.

Planking the food he had ordered in front of him, the redfaced blonde drifted down to the other end to shoot the breeze with a corpulent drummer. Marratt ate with a cautious care, chewing slowly, hearing no mention of himself in the talk around him. One by one the others finished and straggled off to pursuits more personal, the drummer being the last to depart after fixing up a tentative date with the hasher. The cook filled a plate and took a stool at the counter. The blonde picked over some of the stuff on the stove, finally hung up her apron and went out the back door.

The cook swabbed his plate out, picked up Marratt's cup and drew him another coffee. "Never figured you'd come back," he said, setting the smoking beverage in front of him.

Marratt sat perfectly still for the space of one heartbeat, then went on with his chewing, not looking at the man but very conscious of his inspection.

He didn't know what to say hardly, but it began to be apparent he was going to have to say something. The cook hadn't budged and he was still looking at him. Marratt grunted. "Don't they always?"

"I didn't look for you to. I always figured you had a heap too much savvy."

Marratt pushed a crust of bread around the trough of his plate. He put his teeth to work on it while he thoughtfully assayed the cook's words for significance. "Meaning, I guess, you didn't reckon pride —"

"Pride!" The old man snorted. "What did pride ever get your pappy? If it's pride fetched you back you're a goddam fool!"

Scowling with outrage he snatched up his plate and three-four other dirty dishes and dumped them, back of the stove, on the double-barreled two-foot stack in the sink. Taking up a broom he started sweeping the place out. "Pride!" he muttered, swinging the broom with a venomous vigor. But when he reached the counter he glared at Marratt again. "What the hell you fixing to do?"

"I think," Marratt said, "you've mixed me up with someone else."

"You better not try handing that line to Wineglass!"

12

Marratt swallowed the rest of his coffee. He dropped a silver dollar beside his plate and let his eyes play over the cook's scowling face. "Just who do you happen to have me pegged for?"

The old man took a good long look at him. "You've changed some, I'll admit it; but not enough to pull any wool over Wineglass. You look just about the way old Jake did at your age — a lot more like him than you did fifteen years ago. And them whiskers you're growing is a plumb waste of time."

Marratt shook his head. Hoof sound and laughter pounded past on the street outside and he saw the old man stiffen, swivel a quick glance toward the windows. When he brought his face back there was no doubting his sincerity. "Go out the back way, Luke, and mebbe you can get out of town without any of that bunch seein' you."

"But I tell you —"

"Would you involve a defenseless old man in your feuding? Don't argue, you feather-headed dimwit — git goin'!" he rasped harshly, and shoved Marratt doorward.

Marratt stepped out of light into thick felted darkness.

It was commencing to rain. He heard the patter of it round him as the cook slammed the door shut, and a low ground wind carried

13

the smell of it strongly through the additional odors of wet sand and cedar.

Hunching his shoulders, Marratt turned up his collar, knowing the need to get away from this place. There might be no more back of the old man's talk than a desire to hooraw what he took for a down-and-outer, but a fugitive couldn't afford that chance.

He had seen beforehand the very real risks he must expect to encounter if he were forced to approach or go into some town and had planned his escape with these risks well in mind. The Mexican border was hardly a stone's throw south of Yuma but Marratt was not fooled by that mirage of safety. Nor was he tempted into trying one of the several other routes a really clever man might have elected to travel. He had chosen the impossible and gone straight east into the wastes of the desert, convinced this was the only direction no intelligent man would expect him to head for.

He had gone through the Wellton Hills and braved the peaks of the Copper Mountains, the Mohawks and the Eagle Tanks, skirting the northern slopes of the Craters and Saucedas, finally floundering his way across the crags of the Sand Tanks to come into Bella Loma from the south. He had never before been in this part of the country and had reckoned himself reasonably safe from meeting anyone who might know him; he could hardly have expected to be taken for another.

Nor was he satisfied he had been. He found it easier to believe that old cook had been hoorawing him; but whatever the reason behind that old man's talk and actions it plainly behooved Marratt to get the hell away from here as speedily as possible.

He had three sure things in his favor. Before coming into this town at all he'd made sure it had no telegraph. Outlying regions could not be warned to be on the watch for him. The night would conceal his movements and this cold drizzle should wipe out his tracks before morning. So, no matter what was back of that old coot's talk or what he might now be doing about it, the way to escape was still open.

On the debit side of the ledger, however, was the encroaching result of that food he had just taken into his overtaxed half-starved system. The effects were already becoming apparent in the unwonted inertia that was blurring his perceptions. He felt a terrible desire to crawl into some covert and sleep the clock around. He had to fight this with all his resistance. He knew his mind wasn't working with its accustomed precision; the wheels of his thinking had slowed to a snail's pace and it was all he could do to keep his eyes open.

He tipped back his head and let the cold rain beat into his face and it helped some, but the orange shine of those lamp-lighted windows exerted a tremendous attraction; he wheeled with a frightened curse when he found himself clomping toward them. *Get yourself in hand, you goddam fool!*

He broke into a shambling run and the rain-slicked gumbo underfoot sent him sprawling. A kind of panic got into him. He clawed himself upright and hurled a curse into the windy, rain-lashed night and stood glaring about him. Like an animal at bay, he thought bitterly; and started walking. Before he had covered fifty feet of puddled ground the desire to lie down was at work on him again and the lights of a boarding house loomed squarely ahead of him. A dollar a night, said the sign beneath the lantern to the left of the door. He had his hand on the knob when something hammered his right side and flung him halfway around.

He sagged against the wall, squeezing the knob of that door with all the strength he had in him, raking the wet blackness of the street with frantic eyes.

You don't question the shock of lead ripping into you; there's no other feeling like it. Marratt knew he had been shot and was trying to spot the shooter when he realized what

16

a beautiful target he presented crouched beneath that goddam lantern.

He was reaching for it, whirling, when the second shot beat dust from the weathered facing of the doorframe. He flung the lantern into the mud of the road, dropping prone to the boards of the porch as he did so.

The third shot howled above Marratt's head and he heard it plow through the porch rail. That gave him the angle and he caught one brief glimpse of a short and broad shape vanishing around the corner of one of those across-the-street saloons.

He staggered onto his feet, trying to understand the psychology of a community which gave no attention to the racket of gunfire. Not a window had gone up, not a door had been flung open. Nor could he think of any reason for this attempt on the life of a total stranger unless some truth lurked behind that damn cook's jawing and he had again been mistaken for somebody else.

It didn't make sense but he wasn't going to argue. He wasn't going to wait around for any further hints. The quicker he got out of this town the better he'd be suited.

But in the rainswept murk the numbness in his side produced by the shock of the bushwhacker's bullet began to wear away and pain sledged through him in nauseating waves.

The second time he stumbled he latched hold of a tree to steady himself and flung a wondering glance across his left shoulder at the line of racked horses hitched before the saloons.

Bad, however, as he was tempted to try for one, common sense assured him that to show himself now in the light from those windows could too easy turn out to be the same thing as suicide.

Shanks' mare was rough but an unarmed man could find a lot of things rougher.

Chapter 2

He was more used up than he had realized. He had no idea of how long he had been walking or how far he might have come. It all looked the same. Darkness garbed the land with impenetrable curtains and when he stopped, as he sometimes did to listen, there was nothing to be heard beyond the drone of the rain and the gusty slapping of the fitful wind.

Crossing those mountains had taken a lot out of him and this hole in his side wasn't helping matters any. He was chilled to the marrow and unutterably weary. The weight of his sopping store clothes seemed to add an immeasurable burden to the intolerable performance of hoisting one foot and putting it down before the other. It was too remindful of pulling cows out of bog holes.

He lost all count of the times he fell down. It would be simpler, he thought, just to stay down; but always something seemed to prod him onto his feet. If the goddam ground would only stay where it belonged he thought he might be able to keep going, at least until he found some kind of shelter to crawl into.

But everything seemed to conspire against him. When the ground wasn't standing on end to defy him, the whole frilling world was reeling round in a circle and the next thing he'd know he'd be down in the muck again, swearing and puking like a pulque drunk squaw.

Getting up was the hardest but, some way, he always made it. Then he'd stand there awhile trying to get his bearings, swinging his head from side to side like a bull until some-one would jeer: Grete Marratt, you fool, you've reached the end of your rope.

Every time he heard that his stubborn jaws would clamp together and he would go splashing on through the rainswept murk, stumbling and staggering, talking like he was out of his head. *Howl, damn you!* he'd swear at the wind. *Howl your fool guts out and see what that gets you! You ain't stopping Grete Marratt, you son of a bitch!*

There wasn't nobody going to stop Marratt; not, by God, this side of Clagg's partner.

Once he thought he heard buggy wheels, the plop-plopping of hoofs. That was crazy, of course, and he had sense enough to know it. No one but a moron or a fugitive was going to be wandering around in this downpour.

And then he got to thinking he saw the mist-blurred shining of some faroff lamp and he was like some ship-wrecked sailor with his eyes glued on that held-out hope of sanctuary, convinced that he could reach it if the locoed damn thing would have the sense to stay put and not go frisking all over the whole horizon.

Just went to show how wild a mind could get. Like Marratt imagining he saw the gaunt outlines of some kind of shack when any nump would know you couldn't see ten foot ahead of you through these sheeted gusts of wind-driven rain. He seemed to have lost the light now, but he was still floundering toward the shape of that shack when the goddam slop reared up out of the road and slapped him hell west and crooked.

The next impression Marratt had was of hearing those phantom hoofbeats again and the squish-squash-squish of buggy wheels. But when he finally got his mind to where it could pin down the truth he couldn't hear nothing but the slog of the rain. He remembered being on his face again and, centuries later, of hands pawing at him — or maybe it was buzzards. He was too damn tired to look.

When he did open his eyes it wasn't night any more and he reckoned he was out of his head for sure. He appeared to be lying on some sort of a bed in a long narrow room before a burned-down fire that was still throwing warmth. Or maybe it was the sun coming in that west window that had chased the night's damp chill from his marrow. If this were hell he was satisfied. One thing was certain: He'd never been here before.

It wasn't until much later that he began to wonder if he'd made it to the shack — the goddam shack that wasn't there. He reopened one eye cautiously. Somebody'd built the fire up. It was dark beyond the window now and there was a lighted lamp in a wall bracket, turned low but giving the room a yellow radiance brightened and made friendly by the dancing snap and crackle of the burning logs in the fireplace.

He opened the other eye and saw a tumbler of water and a white crockery pitcher placed handy on a chair that he could reach by putting a hand out. By these signs he understood that someone was taking care of him because he sure as hell hadn't done all this himself. It was kind of nice to think that anyone would bother — was, that is, till he recollected who he was.

Realization suddenly hit him with all the

shock of a knee in the groin. It slammed the floodgates of memory wide open. He flung back the blankets someone had put over him and, thoroughly aroused now, was fixing to swing his feet to the floor when pain exploded across his right side with all the breath-gagging nausea of being kicked by a mule.

He sank back white-lipped and trembling and felt cold sweat crack through the pores of his body. That damned bushwhacker's bullet! Alarm spread through him, narrowing his stare as the dangerous implications of his plight unreeled before him. Every instinct of the fugitive warned him to get out of here.

He forced himself to remain perfectly still but he could not control the feverish tumult of his thoughts. He'd been taken in and cared for but you couldn't pin hope on that; even now his unknown benefactor might be summoning a sheriff. How much time had elapsed since he'd been shot in Bella Loma? How much ground had he covered since turning his back on Bella Loma's lights? Where was he now? Where was the person who had fetched him here and how long had that person been gone from the house?

A look at the logs in the fireplace assured him the man hadn't been out of the room long, not over ten or fifteen minutes. He remembered the horse hoofs and buggy wheels then and knew that his Samaritan could not have been a woman for no woman could have lifted him and he sure hadn't gotten here under his own steam.

He'd better try to get up, pain or no pain.

It was only then he discovered he had been undressed. Stripped naked, by God! And no clothes in sight!

That gave him a turn and brought the sweat out again. There was a bandage strapped tight about his ribs but you couldn't go wandering around in a bandage!

He stifled a groan and got an arm beneath his head, hoping it might enable him to locate his clothes. He couldn't see the whole place but he saw enough to know he was in a ranch house and that he was on some kind of couch in what probably passed for the living room.

It didn't seem to have been lived in for a hell of a long while.

Dust lay over everything. Cobwebs hung from the raftered wooden ceiling and were draped from the meager moth-eaten furnishings; webs that hadn't been made yesterday, dark and thick with musty dust.

And then the memory of his nakedness prodded him again and, very carefully, he rolled over and got one foot down solid on the uncarpeted floor preparatory to rising.

With both hands braced firmly under him

he reckoned he could anyways get into a sitting position before his hurt side slugged him into a faint. He could damn well try, and he was going to. Because any gent that would take a fellow's clothes away from him —

He didn't finish the thought because just then he put his hands down and one of them connected with the barrel of a pistol. It was laying on the couch, had been tucked in beneath the blanket. A .45 and fully loaded except, of course, for the single chamber on which the hammer rested.

The weight of that pistol in his hand did wonders for Marratt. It made him feel about seven feet tall and gave him enough gumption to bear the pain of getting onto his feet.

White-cheeked and dizzy, he had just got the blanket wrapped around his middle and was fixing to hunt the house for clothes when he heard the approaching crunch of boots in the gravel outside the room's west door.

Marratt turned, braced the gun against his hip and waited.

The person who opened the door had his left arm piled with groceries. He looked to be crowding sixty; a tall grizzled man in a black alpaca with a black San An tugged low above eyes that flicked toward the couch, fanned outward a little and came swiveling around until they picked up Marratt.

He gave no evidence of being disconcerted. "Expect you're feeling some better," he commented, booting the door shut and fetching his parcels on over to the table. "How's the appetite?"

"Suppose we talk about you."

"Pretty dull subject." The tall man offered a fleeting smile. "You can put that gun down, Luke; I won't bite you."

Marratt said: "Start talking!"

The tall man eyed him a moment longer. But when the hammer clicked back under Marratt's thumb he shrugged and said drily, "All right. What about?"

"About how we got hooked up with each other."

"No mystery about that. I picked you out of the slop of the road during that storm we had here the other night. Been doing the best I can to take care of you —"

"For a price, of course," Marratt's lips turned bitter. He felt weak with standing but he'd got over his dizziness and his mind was at work in some very odd corners. "Get your cards on the table — how much you been hoping to stand me up for?"

Anger darkened the other's cheeks. Then he pushed it away and said coldly to Marratt, "I was hoping the years had taught you something but I guess you haven't changed much, Usher."

"We'll speak of that later. Right now I want to know who you are, what's your angle and why you stuck me in this empty house. I want to know where it is and —"

The tall man, eyeing him incredulously, snorted. "Do you take me for a total fool?"

"I'm going to take you for a target in about ten seconds!"

"All right. I'm Doc Frailey, as you damned well know. Night before last I found you lying unconscious outside the gate. I fetched you here because it was handy, because you happen to own it and because I wasn't at all sure you'd be wanting folks to know you'd come back."

"Any particular reason I wouldn't want them to know it?"

"You're the best judge of that."

"Been away quite a spell, have I?"

Frailey, scowling, finally shrugged and said drily, "Fifteen years."

"And you were able to remember —"

"You took care of that part!"

Marratt said, fishing: "Run out on a bill, did I?"

"Some might be tempted to put it that way."

They considered each other for a couple of

moments. Frailey said impatiently: "I didn't come here to play games, Usher. Put up that —"

"I'm not playing games. I'm trying to get to the bottom of what's going on here; you're not the first to remember me, Frailey."

"I suspicioned as much when I got a look at your side. What the hell did you expect, coming back to this —"

"I must have cut quite a swath to be remembered fifteen years."

Frailey said scornfully, "How long has this amnesia been bothering you?"

Marratt shook his head.

"Have you forgotten telling round how you were going to put a window through Clem Ryerson's skull?"

"So I killed this big mogul and dug for the tules, eh?"

"You never went near him — never even waited for your old man's funeral!"

Marratt's look turned thoughtful. "You know," he said, "Frailey, you *could* be mistaken."

"Hell, I'm not passing judgment. You asked and I told you."

"You haven't yet told how you got onto me so quick."

"It wasn't quick," Frailey sighed. "I had a look at you, of course, soon's I got out of the buggy. Knew I'd seen you before but it was finding you there, not forty yards from this house, that finally put my wheels to churning. Time I'd got you inside and scraped off some of the muck I was pretty damned sure. The picture cinched it."

Marratt's eyes narrowed. "Picture?"

"Old Jake's. Above the couch. You can't miss the resemblance."

Marratt was willing, for the moment, to take his word for it. He went over and sat down. He laid the gun on the chair beside the water glass and pitcher.

"Feeling shakey?" Frailey asked.

"It ain't so much that; I just can't seem . . ." He scrubbed a hand across his eyes. "How bad's this hole in my side?"

"Cracked rib. You'll get over it."

"Why do you reckon I've come back?"

The tall man looked at him sharply, then he glanced at his watch and put it back in his pocket. "I don't know — I don't *want* to know. I don't want any part in it."

"Who was Ryerson? Why did I threaten to kill him?"

The doc studied him quite awhile. "I'd rather you found those things out from someone else —"

"My God," Marratt said, "I've already been shot once! If you didn't think I was in

29

danger why'd you leave me that gun?"

"The gun was here. It belonged to your father."

Marratt, eyeing it, said slowly, "It's been well taken care of."

Frailey shook his head and waved a hand at the wall. "It was hanging in that gun belt. I took it apart. I cleaned it and oiled it." He said on an irritable gust of breath: "Don't ask me why — I just did, that's all!"

A meager smile tugged the corners of Marratt's mouth. "Why hide your light under a bushel, Doc? It was a generous impulse; particularly in a man who thinks as poorly of me as you do."

"I wasn't thinking about you!"

"You must have thought a good deal of Jake Usher then. Did Ryerson kill him?"

Frailey opened his mouth, changed his mind and strode doorward. But halfway there he spun around and came back. "All right, I'll tell you. When you were tanked up on rotgut, and it was doing your talking, you *claimed* Clem Ryerson killed Jake. You were in the Red Horse Bar, yowling what you would do to him. But when they got you sober enough to know wild honey from cow flops you got right into a saddle and commenced laying farapart tracks for the border."

Marratt sighed.

"You had folks on your side up till then," Frailey grumbled. "Now the boot's on the other foot and you're a fool twice over." He puckered his lips up irascibly and spat. "What the hell good did you think coming back would do?"

"Ryerson still alive, isn't he?"

There was a long instant of silence then Frailey said explosively: "You damn well better believe he's alive! His outfit covers almost half of this county — goes clear around you. What Wineglass says is same as law in these sandhills; the marshal's his man just as much as Churk Crafkin."

"Must be a comfortable feeling," Marratt observed, and then asked abruptly: "What am I supposed to do about clothes?"

"I took those old rags of yours out and buried them."

"I'll make quite a hit going around in a blanket."

"There's some of your old things hanging in the closet. Probably be a mite tight —"

"Would you mind fetching a few of them in here? I'll need a pair of boots, too, and a hat while you're at it."

The moment the doctor's back was out of sight Marratt got up and took a look at that picture. He'd been prepared to find a vague likeness in it; a shade of eye, perhaps, a not dissimilar nose. But, staring into that gilt-framed ferrotype, he was almost too astonished to breathe. The pictured face of Jake Usher so closely resembled his own that, except for the sideburns and chin tuft, he might have been looking at a photograph of himself.

He got off weak knees and sagged against the couch's rest with the damndest feeling he had ever experienced. But his mind was made up. There'd be some risk, all right; in fact there'd probably be fireworks — but where better could he hide until the law quit looking than in the clothes and behind the problems Luke Usher had run away from?

Frailey came back with an armful of range clothes which he dumped, with boots and hat, on the couch beside Marratt. "If these don't fit maybe some of Jake's will."

Marratt tried on the boots; a little tight across the sole but he reckoned he could stand it. "How much land have I got here?"

"It's kind of late in the day to start reaching for a halo."

Marratt kept staring till Frailey said testily, "You haven't got a damn inch without Wineglass says so."

"Never mind that. How much was Jake holding onto?"

"Twenty-four thousand acres."

"How come Wineglass didn't take the spread over?"

"They been using it."

"But the books still show it as owned by Usher?"

"Ryerson likes it better that way; he gets the good of it without so much squawk. He don't give a damn who owns it on paper so long as its grass goes into his cattle."

"Then it's legally mine," Marratt said. "Tomorrow —"

"There'll be no tomorrow for you around here. You better take my advice and get out while you're able."

Chapter 3

After Frailey departed, Marratt got himself dressed in an assortment of Usher clothing and scraped together a meal from the staples the doctor had left on the table. He had plenty to think about and he gave the bulk of the evening to it.

One thing he'd probably ought to do right away was to let it be known he'd not returned — in his character of Luke — to make trouble. He was perfectly willing to let sleeping dogs lay and hoped Ryerson might hold a similar conviction.

After all, Marratt argued, it didn't have to be Wineglass that had triggered that shot at him. It could be the cook from the Lone Star Grub, or someone the cook had set onto him. He had no way of guessing what antagonism Luke had kicked up before cold feet had hustled him out of the country.

One thing, however, could almost certainly be banked on: Whoever had tried to cut him down with those bullets was pretty near bound to have another whack at it.

But there were several different ways of looking at this business. And the more Marratt prodded it around in his mind the less inclined he became to feel sure the answer was Wineglass.

On the face of such facts as had been supplied by Doc Frailey certainly Ryerson stood to gain the most by getting rid of Luke Usher. Luke's bolt on the heels of his father's death had already given Wineglass fifteen crops of Usher grass, not to mention the profitable revenue from fifteen crops of abandoned cattle which Ryerson's men had probably branded with impunity. One could not readily imagine Ryerson being willing to abandon the source of such profits.

On the other hand, however, if Wineglass had become as powerful as Frailey's talk had indicated, why should Ryerson have tried to pot his duck from ambush? Why go out on a limb when the obvious thing would have been to laugh in Usher's face?

Bushwhacking, generally, was the resort of a frightened man. What had Ryerson to be afraid of? Why should the owner of Wineglass, controlling local law and presumably backed by a crew of hard-riding rannies, be even mildly perturbed by the return of a man he'd already run out of this country once?

Marratt shook his head. It just didn't make sense. Even assuming Ryerson to be a bit disconcerted by the apparent return of old Jake's spineless son, there would seem little occasion for such drastic measures. Much, of course, might depend on the two men's characters and Marratt realized he knew precious little about either of them — and who was this fellow Doc had called Churk Crafkin? The answer to that attempted drygulching might well lie in the relationship of Usher to Crafkin.

Marratt, scowling into the fire, was uncomfortably aware of the risks he was taking. But better a feud than the steel bars of Yuma. Better the dangers which he saw piled around him than the certainties he'd be facing if he let opportunity's knock go unheeded. He had no horse and damned little money yet, here in Bella Loma in the guise of Luke Usher, he need only face the perils inherent in Usher's name and past entanglements. On the dodge as a fugitive, every man's hand would be turned against him. Here he faced only the threat of individuals; in flight he'd be surrounded by all the multiple and ever-vigilant resources of the law.

All his thoughts in prison had been concentrated on escape, on getting outside where he could search for Clagg's partner. Now, having escaped and reacquainted himself with liberty, life had become suddenly dear to him again and the likelihood of coming across the man he was hunting almost hopeless. Clagg's partner — like Clagg himself — had been a stranger to the country around Prescott. Marratt had no means of knowing where the man had come from and those five years he'd spent at Yuma had not freshened the trail up any. The description he'd gotten of the fellow's appearance indicated a certain prosperity and his horse had been rigged in the manner of desert travel; beyond this all Marratt had as clues to work with were the few things Charlie had mentioned — that three-fingered hand, an uptilted nose and the knife scar across a left temple. Not much to go on with the hounds of the law in full cry all about him. But if he could stick it out here until the law became engrossed in matters more urgent and he had got himself accepted indisputably as Luke Usher, why then he might be able to go after that guy in earnest.

He got up and turned around and had another long look at Jake Usher's pictured features. The resemblance was uncanny. Usher had the same stubborn sweep of jaw, the same sandy hair, dark inscrutable eyes and lean gash of a mouth which had looked back at

Marratt from countless fords and mountain pools while the horse had been dropping its head to water.

And speaking of horses, Marratt reflected, he had better put his brain to the task of promoting one. He certainly hadn't the price in his pocket and a fellow caught afoot in cow country was uncommon likely to be regarded askance.

His mind had just winged back to that corral he'd seen in town when he suddenly tensed, hand dropping to gun butt, as hard knuckles pounded the outside of the door. He cleared the gun for action, got back to the couch and called: "Come in."

The man who shoved open the door was a study in contradictions.

Marratt had been halfway expecting to see the face of that cook or the short and broad shape of the one who had tried to cut him down the other night. This bird was a stranger. He was garbed in a blue-and-white striped shirt, open at the throat, and the bottoms of his corduroy trousers were thrust into fancy-topped Hyer boots — which don't grow on bushes. A black curly-brimmed Stetson was shoved back off the forehead of a long narrow face that, from the nose on down, was sheathed in black beard.

But no beard was going to conceal his pleasure in greeting a friend he hadn't seen in fif-teen years. He came in like a wriggling collie with hand outstretched and teeth shooting splinters of light through the bristle. "How are you, son —"

His voice suddenly forgot the good will it was building and went into a bleat as he caught sight of the snout of that motionless pistol. "Great Gawd a'mighty, Luke! Put that dratted thing away — you ain't forgot Clint Gainor, hev you? Ol' Clint that learned you how to set a buckin' bronc — Gee-rusalem! I —"

"Close the door," Marratt said without change of expression. "Now come around here into the light where I can see you and don't make no sudden passes."

Gainor followed instructions, sideling into the downturned glow from the lamp like a drunk on a chalkline. There was something strangely ineffectual about his big-bellied shape, a suggestion of timidity he'd probably hoped to hide — and maybe generally did — behind that bluff hail-fellow-well-met air of heartiness he'd been so busily exuding as he'd stepped over the threshold.

Marratt put up his gun but kept a hand close beside it. "How'd you know I was here?"

"Perkins — he cooks for the Lone Star —

39

was tellin' me he seen you and then, about a hour ago, I run into Doc — Hell's fire, boy! Don't you remember Ol' Clint what wrassled steers for your pappy down to Keeler's Crossin' that time the Mesca—"

"Sure. Vaguely," Marratt decided. "But I can't seem to recollect us ever getting so close for you to come busting a gut to get over here the minute you learn I'm back in the country. And so spider-footed quiet —"

"I kin tell you about that —"

"What'd you do with your horse?"

Gainor licked his lips while a slow flush spread through his haired-over jowls. "I'm goin' to tell you about that — it's all part of the same thing, of the reason for my bein' here. I guess maybe you got some call to be wonderin', but it sure ain't what you think. I've had to play my cards mighty close these last years. You don't want to believe more'n half of what you hear —"

"All right," Marratt said. "I've got the salt box handy. Get down to brass tacks."

Gainor stared. He said defensively, "I dunno what you've heard but what I've done's been 'cause I've had to. It ain't been easy to live around here I kin tell you with Wineglass knockin' right ag'in my east fence. Let Clem Ryerson hev his way an' he'll glom onto this whole country from the Sierra

Estrellas clean to Pozo Redondo — an' don't you never think he won't!"

"We'll let that stand as said, for the moment. Let's hear about the reason you came hiking over here. And why you didn't ride up like a neighbor."

Gainor's look turned reproachful. "You know mighty well I can't afford to neighbor with Ushers. Now don't get me wrong! You might not hev guessed it but I've always kinda nourished a secret likin' for you, boy. I'm one of the few around this patch of cactus that never figured you pulled out account of bein' scairt o' Wineglass."

"That so?" Marratt allowed himself to unbend a little. "Why did you think I pulled my freight?"

" 'Cause you was too damn smart to go ag'in a stacked deck."

"The line separatin' smartness from cowardice ain't much easier to latch hold of than the hair on a frog. You must have a good pair of eyes."

"I got 'em," Gainor nodded, "an I kin put two an two together. Lots of guys — most all of 'em — what heard them cracks you made in the Red Horse Bar that night figured it was the whisky talkin', but I knowed better. I knowed you meant every dad-gummed word of it — an' that's what's fetched me over here now. I knowed damn well you was aimin' to come back an' I've been buildin' toward that time."

He grinned felinely through the brush of his whiskers. "I kin see you think I'm just butterin' you up. Don't you believe it, boy. I'm here to do my Christian duty an' you a good turn at the same time mebbe."

Marratt watched the sly eyes go from himself to Jake's picture. "Put your cards on the table."

But it wasn't in Gainor's roundabout nature to travel the shortest way if he could avoid it. "How much dough hev you got?" he asked.

"Do I look like a bake shop?"

"I mean money — hard cash."

"I couldn't stake you to a hairpin."

"What I figured," Gainor nodded. "You ain't even got a horse. Doc said the clothes you was wearin' —"

"You come over here to crow at me?"

"Just pointin' out where you stand is all. Matter of fact, I'm here to help you —"

"You reckon you'll get round to it before morning?"

Gainor managed a parched smile. "You hadn't oughta begrudge me a little mite of time; you're in a bad hole, boy, an' I'm fixin' to pull you out. I'll give you six thousand dollars for the title to this ranch."

Marratt looked at the man and grinned without speaking.

Gainor squirmed around inside his clothes and looked flustered. "All right — I'll give you eight!"

"Eight thousand dollars for twenty-four thousand acres. You call that pulling me out of a hole?"

"You ain't got no twenty-four thousand acres; all you've got's the goddam title!"

"What about Jake's cattle?"

"How many can you produce?"

"That remains to be seen. I can always send Ryerson a bill for what's missing."

Gainor snorted. "You kin fly a kite, too, but what good'll it do you? Way things stand right now you couldn't get six cents on the dollar for this place with Wineglass riders workin' four sides of it an' Winglass cattle gobblin' up the grass! For Chrissake talk sense!"

Marratt said coldly, "The only way it makes sense you'd give me eight thousand dollars for the deed to this spread presupposes you're convinced I've come back to kill Ryerson. I haven't; but on that basis — and providing I was able to get the job done — you'd have title to a property worth around eight times what it cost you. Not to mention any cattle you might be able to round up."

43

Angry color jumped into Gainor's scowling cheeks. "So what if I did figure it that way?" he blustered. "No skin off your nose! You can't use the place anyway. You got no money to stock it — no way of gettin' Ryerson's stock off. Even with the cash to do it you couldn't get a crew that would go up ag'in' Wineglass. If you funk killin' Ryerson he'll run you outa the country. If you avenge your pappy, like any guy with a lick o' gumption *would* do, you'll still hev to run. So what good's this place to you?"

His eyes ran over Marratt shrewdly. "Be reasonable, Luke. If I'm willin' to take the gamble you oughta be glad to hev me do it. A guy can't pick that kinda money off the bushes." He said persuasively, "Once you're across the border a stake like that'll set you up like a king. Think of the women it'll buy — the whisky — the *mozos*. Christ, I'm almost tempted to go down there myself!"

He got out a roll of banknotes and counted eight thousand down onto the table, stood peering at Marratt smugly. "There it is. All I want is your name on a quitclaim."

"Yes," Marratt thought, that was really all he wanted. He didn't give a damn what Luke decided to do afterwards.

Gainor, obviously knowing more about Luke than Marratt had, produced a flask from his pocket and set it down on the table beside that thick sheaf of currency. "Reckoned you might like a nip —"

The oily smile suddenly whisked out of sight in Gainor's whiskers as he fell back in alarm before the look of Marratt's eyes.

"Pick up your bottle and your money," Marratt said, coming off the couch, "and get outside that door before my temper gets away from me."

Chapter 4

Several afternoons later Marratt, getting out of the saddle before the administration offices at the Malicora agency, left the horse Doc Frailey had hired for him on grounded reins beside a similarly anchored head-tossing bay filly. Stepping onto the porch he slanched a casual glance at the silent Indian solemnly squatted behind the sweltering folds of a red wool blanket. "Agent in?"

The Maricopa's eyes rolled up at him indifferently and as indifferently returned to contemplation of the faroff mountains.

Marratt pulled open the screen door and stood a moment just inside accustoming his eyes to the drawn-blind dimness by which the agent was attempting to modify the heat. There was no one in this cramped waiting room but a shadowy corridor, leading off to the left, revealed a door standing open. Marratt, gravitating toward it, heard a fluttering of papers.

The cavity beyond the door turned out to be a quite spacious office. Dust-covered Indian artifacts were arranged on boards hung about the walls and products of Indian industry, equally dusty, were heaped on tables below them and stacked without care in obscure corners. A comely squaw in a beaded headband looked up from a desk to say "Yes?" and Marratt told her that, if possible, he'd like to have a talk with the agent.

"Stanley Beckwith," she said. "He'll be back in a moment," and, extricating several slips from the sheaf she'd been going through, rubber-banded the rest and dropped them into a drawer which she closed. Picking up the others she went off down the hallway.

Pretty efficient, Marratt thought, and wondered where Beckwith had found himself a squaw with sufficient education to serve as office help.

He dropped into a chair and sat with his thoughts picking over other talks he'd recently had with Indian agents and hoping, by God, this one was going to be different. Leather heels coming down the corridor drew him out of this thinking and pulled his eyes toward the door.

The man who came in was stoop-shouldered, tall, and so thin he'd have to stand twice to cast a shadow. The skin of his

47

face was like yellowed parchment in the blind-filtered light coming in through the window as, with a querulous glance, he gave Marratt a nod and said, "Well? What is it?"

Marratt kept his seat. "I'm looking for Stanley Beckwith, the agent."

"You've found him," the tall man grunted, gingerly lowering his bones into the padded desk chair. "I've no range to lease if that's what you're here for."

"Thought, perhaps," Marratt said, "you might be needing some beef."

The agent looked as though he were about to say no but, as his mouth came open, something changed his mind. He picked up a penknife and got to work on his nails. "What . . . ah . . . kind of beef?"

"Cheap," Marratt growled, and Beckwith turned that over awhile but instead of asking *how* cheap he said without glancing up from his nail job; "Anyone suggest this agency to you?"

"Just occurred to me you might need some."

"Customarily we purchase beef supplies by contract —"

"I know all that. I've sold beef to Indian agencies before."

"In that case you'll understand our funds are rather limited. Which reservations have you been doing business with?"

Marratt said, fed up with this fencing, "This beef is priced right. Can you use it now or can't you?"

He knew as soon as the words were spoken he'd used the wrong tone with this fellow.

Beckwith's look turned cagey. "Where are you getting this beef?"

"Where do you suppose I'm getting it? From my own spread, naturally."

"Naturally." Beckwith smiled. "Now suppose you tell me with what iron it is branded."

"Do you find certain brands to be more palatable than others?"

Beckwith managed a rusty chuckle. He laid aside the penknife and pyramided his fingers into the shape of a steeple. "We are forced to be very careful what kind of beef we feed to the Indians. Our buying powers are fenced with restrictions. It might be, however, that at some later date —"

"Look," Marratt said, "I've got some beef to sell now; I don't know what I'll have later. I might close out this ranch and go somewhere else. I'm not trying to hurry you into a deal but if you can't use this stuff just say so."

Beckwith peered at him uncertainly, wanting the cattle but scared to stick his neck out. Marratt understood the man's dilemma. The Indian Service was notoriously underpaid; if he could get these cattle cheap enough he could pad out his income by putting the difference in his pocket. He wanted like hell to do it but he had to be sure there wouldn't be any comeback. "Are you willing to guarantee — I mean to put it down in writing — you're the sole and legal owner of every steer you're offering to sell me?"

"I'm putting nothing on paper. On the other hand," Marratt said, "I'm willing to produce local residents who have known me for upwards of twenty years and will verify my right to dispose of the beef in question."

"Reputable residents?"

"That will be for you to say. I'll name them when you agree to do business."

"What do you call 'cheap'?"

"Will you pay seven dollars a head?"

Beckwith's eyes gleamed. Sweat broke through the skin of his face and he was starting to get up when worry dropped him back again. The price was too low. Beckwith said suspiciously, "You couldn't afford to sell steers of your own raising —"

"I never said they were of my raising. As a matter of fact I have just come into them. The reason I'm practically giving you these cattle is because without your help I couldn't round them up nor attempt to make delivery. I'd have to borrow some of your Indians —"

"I couldn't let you do that. I'm not permitted —"

"Why couldn't we work it out this way? You send a crew down there and hold your own roundup. I'll be available to identify the cattle. When you've made your gather, drift them up here and pay me seven bucks a head for whatever you arrive with. That's fair enough, ain't it?"

The agent said with a fishy stare, "Why can't you —"

"Because I haven't any crew."

"Then how do you know you've anything to sell?"

Marratt got up. "Hell with you," he said.

He was partway through the door when Beckwith's discontented voice plowed after him. "Wait —"

Marratt wheeled.

"I might take them at five."

"You're not the only flower on this dunghill. There are other agencies," Marratt reminded him.

Greed in Beckwith was still clawed by fear but you could see Marratt's price making weight in the balance. The man couldn't bear to think of losing such profit. He stood squirming and trembling on the verge of acceptance when a last jab from caution prodded him into asking, "Where do I go for these cattle?"

"Vekol Wash, south and east of Bella Loma."

Beckwith looked like a sledge had struck him. His face turned green. His eyes bugged like they would roll off his cheekbones. "That's Wineglass range!"

"They can't stop you from picking up Usher cattle."

"Ush— *Merciful God!*" Beckwith collapsed like a ruptured sack.

Marratt returned.

The agent cringed. He flung up an arm. "Go away — go away," he gasped, whimpering.

"For Christ's sake, what ails you?"

Beckwith moaned. When Marratt stepped nearer he ground bony shoulders into the chair back.

Marratt, fastening a hand in the front of his shirt, hauled him onto his feet. "Answer me, damn you!" He cuffed Beckwith's face until some of the crazed terror fell out of the agent's stare. "Start working your jaws!"

"There —" Beckwith shuddered. "There ain't no Usher cattle."

"Why not?"

But Marratt already knew without Beckwith telling him that what hadn't died from natural causes had sure as hell gone to stuff Indian bellies out of contracts filled by Clem Ryerson's Wineglass.

With a snort of disgust he flung the agent away from him.

How long he'd been riding or how far he had come to where he was now Marratt had no idea when the dog's growl riveted his horse in its tracks. They'd been about to move into a thick growth of willow and the dog stood before it, growling through the folds of what he held in his teeth.

Marratt's horse blew a gusty breath through its nostrils. It danced to one side and the dog growled again. He was just a big overgrown shaggy-haired pup, a typical Indian cur by the look of him. Marratt spoke to him softly and the dog wagged his tail. Just a little, that is. He kept watching them belligerently, not moving from his tracks.

Marratt stared a bit more carefully at what the pup was holding. It seemed to be some kind of buckskin shirt. "Your boss," Marratt said, "is going to whale the hair off you." Alert for a rush he swung out of the saddle. "Where'd you get that?" he asked, holding out his hand.

The dog loosed another growl and stood bristling. But when Marratt squatted down, not going any closer, the big pup let go of the beautifully tanned leather and with a tentative tail wag proceeded cautiously to approach.

Marratt remained still while the dog sniffed over him. Then the pup put his panting face on Marratt's knee and, receiving the pleasurable touch of friendly fingers, rolled over to let the man scratch his chest.

Marratt did, and picked up the shirt as he got to his feet. The dog jumped to grab it but flattened, tail thumping weeds, when Marratt ordered him down. "I think," Marratt said, "we'd best take this thing back before somebody gets into trouble."

That suited the pup. He darted off through the trees. Marratt, following, let his mind slide back to his talk with Clint Gainor. He was unprepared for the blue-gray look of the gleaming dug tank which suddenly confronted him. He was even less prepared for the lovely naked figure that abruptly went splashing into it.

When she again broke surface she was out in the middle and not in any mood to be reserving her opinions. She still had the beaded headband around her dripping hair and her eyes — brown or black — were flashing with bitter outrage. "What do you think you're doing around here?"

Marratt felt like a fool. It was the girl from

Beckwith's office. "I — I wasn't figuring to spy on you. I —"

"Not much, you weren't! You despicable polecat!"

"Lordy, ma'am, I had no idea —"

"Then why did you follow me? Let go of my dress, you grinning hyena, and start making tracks before I —"

"Dress!" Marratt stared blankly at the fringed piece of buckskin. He was utterly astounded. He supposed it *could* be a dress at that, now she'd mentioned it. "Golly," he said, "I —"

"Spare me your lies. Just put it down and go away."

"But I thought it was a shirt — a man's hunting shirt," he explained. "The dog —"

"*What* dog!"

Marratt, to his considerable consternation, discovered the pup had vanished. He peered helplessly about, feeling and probably looking as big a hypocrite as she thought him. He even loosed a couple of half-hearted calls, hoping the dog might put in an appearance, while the girl's scathing eyes stared with angry contempt.

Finally, in desperation, he told her how he'd encountered the dog and how he'd happened to arrive in this clearing, but he could see she wasn't believing a word of it.

"All right," she said when he'd finished, "what are you hanging around for now? Are you intending to wait till I come out of the water?"

"Christ, no!" Marratt gasped with cheeks flaming. He whirled in confusion, made a dive for the trees, and heard a tremendous splashing behind him. Sweat poured through the pores of his skin. Was that damned girl actually coming out of the tank?

He risked a look, found she was, and broke into a run.

"Come back here, you dadburned low-down hypothecator!"

But Marratt wasn't wanting any more of her tongue. He redoubled his efforts and came out of the trees panting to find his horse looking at him with a palpable astonishment. It wasn't till he started to swing into the saddle that he realized he still had her dress in his hand.

He stared at it blankly and then with a curse flung it down and got out of there. He had troubles enough without getting tangled in any squabbles with Indians! He hoped she would find it but he'd be damned if he was going to wait around to make sure.

Chapter 5

All the way home Marratt angrily tried to concentrate his mind on the talk he'd had with that conniving agent but his exasperating thoughts kept sneaking off to the girl he had found in Beckwith's office. Mostly his recollections were of how she had looked going into that tank; though there was one part, too, about the look of her coming out that persisted in taking up a lot of his attention.

Her voice, he remembered, had been unexpectedly deep, not mannish at all but a kind of bright contralto that would have made a carven image turn around for another look. She had the blackest hair he had ever encountered; the whitest teeth, most eloquent eyes, the longest legs and captivatingest pair of —

"Hell!" he snarled through a growl of disgust, and tried again, scowling fiercely, to cuff his thoughts back to Beckwith.

She probably wasn't, he decided, more than seventeen or eighteen, but if you cared for Indian models she'd come off the topmost shelf. And she hadn't been hid in any hogan when the brains were being passed out or Beckwith wouldn't have had her working around his office.

Something queer about that deal anyway because, generally, white collar jobs around an agency were given to widows or elderly spinsters when the Service didn't have any spare males available.

He had never heard of the government hiring squaws in any capacity and you'd have thought that rabbity agent would have been a heap too careful to go hiring one on his own hook — even so delectable a one as he appeared to have latched onto. It got Marratt to wondering all over again how they had managed to get acquainted and if there might not be something more between them than was immediately apparent.

He found this notion strangely repugnant and sought uncomfortably to find out why it should bother him. Beckwith's morals — or hers, for that matter — were certainly no concern of Grete Marratt's. It surely wasn't an interest in the girl herself that was prodding him . . . or was it?

Thoroughly disquieted he scowled at the horn of his saddle.

He had never considered himself to be

much different from the average run of fellows brought up in cow country. He had known a few women, two or three of them intimately, but when he'd driven that slug between Clagg's bulging eyes he'd renounced further right to normal relationships. And he sure wasn't about to set up as a squaw man.

So far as that went — and he was positive of this much — he had no right to the regard of any woman. Not with the law trying to pick up his trail.

He was able on that thought to put her out of his mind for the moment and to go over somewhat sketchily the gist of his conversation with Beckwith.

The man was a puling self-confessed crook who had knowingly bought Usher cattle from Wineglass, secure in the presumption of Ryerson's local influence.

Marratt, with customary thoroughness, had already tackled the other roundabout agencies without discovering any interest in stock which could be had on terms substantially beneath the current market value. Wineglass contracts, he'd been pointedly informed, were amply taking care of all the beef their money was able legally to purchase.

He had never seriously intended trying to unload Usher cattle although he had, to be sure, briefly pondered the possibilities. What he had been after was the knowledge just un-covered, an Indian Agent's duplicity which he could, if he were forced to, hold over Ryerson's head.

He hadn't, of course, any proof that would stand up if it came to a lawsuit, nor did he imagine such proof existed, but he was strongly inclined to doubt that Wineglass would court a public inquiry. His obvious course should things start getting rough would be to have a talk with Ryerson and give the man to understand he'd placed written particulars in other folks' hands to be exam-ined in the event he happened to turn up dead or missing.

It wasn't the best defense in the world be-cause a bullet might catch him before he ever got to Ryerson. It might be smarter, he de-cided, to seek out Ryerson right away; the only trouble with this idea was that it might take a deal of doing. Undoubtedly Ryerson had heard Luke Usher was back and it seemed equally believable he would have taken precautions to make sure the fellow had no chance to get near him.

The girl swung Marratt's thoughts once again in the direction of Beckwith and on a sudden hunch he stopped his horse and de-voted several moments to a frowning specula-tion. Moved by the result of this thinking he sent the horse obliquely north and after twenty minutes of hard-pushed riding he pulled the gelding into a more comfortable lope and commenced to look round for sign.

He could be entirely wrong but, considering the man's character and the jolt he'd received, it appeared to Marratt quite likely that at the earliest opportunity the jittery agent would light out by the shortest route for Wineglass.

Through careful questioning of Frailey, Marratt had a pretty good idea of the approximate location of Ryerson's headquarters. This was the knowledge which had hurried him north hoping to intersect the line of Beckwith's probable travel. After another fifteen minutes he discovered a trail that looked likely and when he came onto it he found ample evidence that someone had used it within the last hour. Someone headed west and in a hell of a hurry.

He had no reason to doubt this was Beckwith. The man was in a sweat to reach Ryerson and Marratt didn't know if he'd best follow him or not, finally deciding to follow him far enough to make certain this hunch was paying bonafide dividends and not sidetracking him down some blind alley.

If these tracks were made by a horse packing Beckwith and the agent was actually making for Wineglass it behooved Grete Marratt to find a hole to crawl into until he could arrange to have that talk with the cow king. It wasn't hard at all to imagine Ryerson's reactions once he learned the supposed Usher was on the trail of those vanished cattle.

Marratt took a quick look at his shadow, rapidly calculated how much longer he could expect to have daylight, and set out on the trail of the hurrying hooftracks.

He rode leisurely now, giving himself time for thought, seriously wondering if he had made the right choice in deciding to pass himself off for Luke Usher. There was so much he didn't know. . . .

He might have dug some of these things out of Beckwith if he'd thought of it — he might still. But further thought tended to persuade him it would be too risky to overtake the agent within striking distance of Ryerson's headquarters. They'd have the whole crew out hunting him and, with superior knowledge of the country, would have him bottled up in no time. No, his best bet now was simply to make sure the agent was carrying his story to Ryerson.

Marratt had concluded there would no longer be any proof of what had happened to the Usher cattle; now he was inclined to question this assumption. Some of the Wineglass crew who had been in on the drives which had taken that beef to Beckwith might still be around.

He wished the hell he knew more about Luke's character, about the fellow's habits and personal mannerisms. By the way he had run you might suspect him of a broad stripe of yellow where he should have had a backbone, but Marratt dared not depend even on this. This drygulcher evidently hadn't considered Luke a coward. By Doc Frailey's telling, however, Luke had got blind drunk after his father's killing and had then pulled his freight without even attempting to make good on his brags.

Marratt stopped his horse of a sudden, eyes narrowing. The plain trail he'd been following had just come over a section of ledgerock which in turn had given way to a stretch of loose shale as it left the dry bed of a once-a-year river. He was still on the trail but the fresh tracks had vanished. He scanned the line of old willows bordering each bank and then glanced back at the ford, not liking this a little bit.

Why had Beckwith quit the trail? Where was he now? In those willows someplace watching Marratt across a rifle?

Marratt's frowning stare angled back across the wash to where the trail curled down off the flank of a ridge, striving to recall if Beckwith's tracks had come down also. But they must have else Marratt would not have entered the wash himself. They must have quit the trail as it crossed that ledge.

If somehow Beckwith had discovered he was being followed and was now concealed and watching within the cover of those willows it would be the height of folly to show an interest in his tracks. To cast around for sign would almost certainly fetch a bullet; even now the flesh was cringing between Grete Marratt's shoulders.

He swung down, pretending to be tightening the girth of his saddle. He stretched then and yawned and took a cursory glance at the lowering sun which seemed about to drop behind the Maricopa Mountains. The feel of eyes was strong in Marratt as he climbed back into his saddle and sent the gelding foxtrotting forward into the unscuffed trail.

He did not look back but kept his glance unostentatiously employed with scanning the landscape ahead of him, seeking to find a place where he could leave the trail himself. There very obviously wasn't any, not in the next couple of miles which stretched before him flat as a table. A number of big boulders farther along constricted his vision and there was a scattering of gnarled mesquites but nothing which might serve as a competent screen for departure.

It seemed impossible Beckwith could have discovered him for at no time had he caught sight of the man or even heard sound of his travel. It seemed a deal more likely the harried agent had simply got off the trail at the best opportunity, hoping thus to outfox any possible pursuit.

He must be getting, Marratt decided, uncomfortably close to Ryerson's headquarters. Another three or four miles should be giving him sight of the buildings. The sun was gone, dropped behind those purple crags, and dusk would soon be unrolling its sables. He resolved to cut south as soon as he could.

He reached the first boulder and put it behind him. He passed several others and was rounding the last of these miniature buttes, observing how the land dipped beyond into greasewood, when he discovered fresh tracks beneath the gelding's feet. These curled in from the right and were without question the ones he'd been following and lost at the river.

So Beckwith *had* been attempting to mislead pursuit. And he was still bound for Wineglass.

Marratt, bending from the saddle to closer scrutinize the sign, was suddenly frozen in the posture when a lifting breeze fetched the sound of a hard-pushed horse from behind him. The dim clatter of shod hoofs on that ledge was unmistakable.

He was out of the saddle in the flash of an eye, leaving the gelding rooted on dropped reins. Snatching off Usher's hat he ducked round the butte until, down on his belly, he could catch the dark line of the willows and a low-crouched rider coming pellmell out of them.

He watched the oncoming animal for several wondering moments, seeing the shape of it grow and become clearer. Though he could not make out the rider it was apparent the man was traveling this trail and that, before very long, he was going to come tearing around this butte.

Wriggling cautiously backward Marratt got to his feet. He resumed Usher's hat and, not drawing his gun but regathering the reins, held his horse by its cheekstrap, his free hand lightly placed across its quivering nostrils.

A man didn't usually travel hellity larrup without he was hunting a sawbones or doing his damndest to outride a sheriff. Marratt did not know what was driving this fellow but he had no intention of being seen if he could help it. Not by anybody bound for Ryerson's Wineglass.

A small stand of salt cedar fringed the

butte's right flank and when the pounding hoofs of the rocketing rider reached the zenith of that building crescendo of sound Marratt led his horse into these and, swiftly turning, got one quick look as the man flashed past.

He stared incredulously after him, jaw sagging in astonishment. He said, "I'll be damned!" for the man on that foam-flecked arrow of horseflesh was Stanley Beckwith, the Indian Agent!

Chapter 6

It didn't seem possible Marratt could have been overtaken by the man whose sign he'd been all this while following. When he got over his surprise Marratt knew it wasn't. He had just seen Beckwith — that much he was sure of. Whose, then, were the tracks he had spent so much time on?

It didn't, perhaps, make so very much difference but Marratt's penchant for thoroughness wouldn't accept such an answer. He'd roughly an hour left of daylight and if it lay within his power he meant to find out.

When he had rammed his feet into Luke Usher's boots he had assumed, along with the identity, all the consequences attendant on Usher's past entanglements. He felt certain it was no coincidence that two separate riders in so short a time should have come this way in such a hell of a hurry. There had to be a connection of some sort between them and, caught up in this now, Marratt had to see it through. Waiting only until Beckwith's shape was lost in the tossing sea of that windwaved greasewood, he came back into the trail and carefully examined the two sets of tracks; the only similarity was that both had been made by fast-moving horses. Speed had gouged them deep into the earth and the ones he'd been following were smaller than the agent's — narrower, probably made by a number 2 shoe.

This, in Marratt's experience, was plain indication of a cleaner-bred mount. The sign left by Beckwith's were the tracks of a puddingfoot.

When he'd first come onto them Marratt hadn't thought of back-tracking this smaller set; he'd been too sure he was on Beckwith's trail to see any point in it. Now he wished he had done so, at least for a way; because, all things considered, he was pretty well convinced he'd been observed by that fellow — that it was this which had occasioned the man's desire for haste. That business at the river practically clinched this assumption and the two, taken together, strongly suggested Marratt had been recognized.

He swung into the saddle and, despite an increasing feeling of uneasiness, again took up the trail. Why had that fellow been so anxious to avoid him?

Forty rods from the butte the small tracks quit the trail and went digging off toward a low ridge adorned with the flaming blossoms of wolf's candle. Marratt, scowling goodbye to Beckwith, followed.

The man had gotten too much of a start by now for there to be any chance of Marratt overtaking him, but there was a slim possibility that he might, with good luck, catch sight of him. Failing that, by grab, Marratt was determined to discover the fellow's destination.

He lifted the big gelding into a run. These tracks weren't over twenty minutes old, grass in some places was just beginning to straighten; and he still had a good bit of fair light left. When he'd first reached that butte where he'd picked up the sign again he must have been right on that jasper's heels. The guy had lost time fooling around in that wash.

They crested the ridge and went down into a trough that was cross-hatched with timber. The tracks slowed here as though the fellow had been aware of Marratt's nearness and had been scared to push his horse lest Marratt hear.

Marratt sailed right along with the gelding wide open. If he could just see this hombre he might learn a lot of things. The guy was paralleling the trail taken by Beckwith or appeared to be, at least, until he reached the valley's end. Then his tracks dived into a kind of shallow canyon whose floor was grown to prickly pear and mounded with the burrows of gophers. These had slowed the fellow further but Marratt didn't let them interfere a bit with his own pace.

He was having more luck than he had imagined possible. That rannyhan couldn't be more than ten minutes ahead of him; they were cutting down his lead with every thud of the gelding's hoofs.

The canyon walls fell away. They crossed a stretch of dwarf cedar, followed the small shoes' sign through a brush-choked ravine which gave onto a darkening gulch angling west in the direction of Wineglass.

Marratt pulled up in the thickening shadows, dubious about going nearer to Ryerson's. If that were this rider's destination after all it might be smarter to let the son-of-a-gun go than risk bumping into the Wineglass crew.

It was while he was stopped, thus considering, Marratt caught the low growl of an angry voice.

Eyes narrowing, he came out of the saddle. They — for a fellow wouldn't be likely to waste that tone on himself — were in this gulch and not far ahead of him. If the man he'd been trailing had come here to meet someone, and Marratt were able to make out their faces and possibly overhear a little, he believed it might strengthen his hand immeasurably.

It was worth a try anyhow!

So, leaving the gelding, he commenced snaking forward, ears cocked and eyes wary, through the green sheen of oak brush, making all the haste possible commensurate with caution.

He didn't know whom he was expecting to encounter but the long narrow face and sly eyes of Clint Gainor weren't far from his thinking as he followed the gulch's inconsistent convolutions, skirting old rock slides and keeping off the direct trail as much as he was able.

He hadn't caught any talk for the last several moments and worried they might have heard him; this being the only explanation he could find for such quiet without they'd finished their business and gone off entirely.

Grown reckless with this last thought, and with no sound for guidance, he shoved through a ten-foot stand of brush and, without warning, was upon them. They stood caught together — one lithely slender, the other short and chunky — before the farther-off shapes of their ground-hitched horses. In the apparent ardor of their embrace the nearer, chunky hombre almost wholly concealed his companion and it wasn't until, with a desperate wrench of slim shoulders, she got one hand loose and tried to get at his pistol that Marratt realized the brawny one had hold of a woman.

Neither one had heard him. The shadows were deepening and Marratt hung there uncertainly a couple of heartbeats before the true significance of their postures registered. It took him that long to untrack his mind from the accepted misconception that, because she must have been awaiting him, she welcomed the man's attentions. But when he saw the fellow, growling, cuff her hand away from his belt gun, Marratt flung himself forward.

Through a red fog of anger he caught the man by the nearest shoulder and spun him around with a berserk fury. His sledging right fist exploded against the man's jaw, sending him crazily staggering slanchways as though he'd crashed into the end of a maul.

It wasn't till then Marratt saw the girl fully, the torn buckskin dress, the dusky pallor of frightened features framed by jet braids as she involuntarily clutched the ripped leather against the pale gleam of an uncovered breast.

He stood rooted in the astonishment of complete incredulity, knowing her now for the girl of the tank — for the Circe of

Beckwith's office. A clamor of questions hammered his mind and his churning thoughts failed entirely to comprehend the utter urgence of the occasion until the girl's cry snatched his glance from her face to pick up the tag end of the man's blurred reach for gun butt.

Marratt threw himself toward him and a bit to the right, at the same time dropping his chest toward his knees as the whistle of lead screamed above his left shoulder. With the man's wrist flexing to shake out another shot Marratt's lifting boot tore the gun from his fingers. He was reeling, half upright, when Marratt's fist landed with the sound of a pile-driver just below his left ear. He went spread-eagled and skidding across the clatterous shale.

When Marratt looked for the girl she was gone with both horses, the hard-drumming impact of their hoofs tumbling off the gulch walls in brittle shatters of sound.

Marratt, rubbing the knuckles of his bruised fist, went over and stood awhile considering the now slack-jawed features of the slugged squaw molester. He had burnt-dark cheeks that were highboned and solid as the muscles that bulged the whole short and broad shape of him. His hat lay brim-up against the base of a juniper and his black hair

74

was straight as a Papago Indian's.

But this was no Indian, Papago or other kind. He looked like a transplanted Texican to Marratt with his lowslung shell belt and grease-grimed opentopped thong-fastened holster. Scowling down at the man Marratt was almighty glad those big knobs of hands hadn't managed to lay hold of him. Strength enough there to snap bones like pipestems.

On a random thought he bent and picked up the man's crown-dented headgear. He hadn't reckoned there'd be one chance in a thousand the battered felt would reward him, but it did. There, burned into the gommy-feeling sweatband with a bit of hot wire, was the bravo's handle: Churk Crafkin. A monicker Marratt had come across before.

Was it Gainor who'd spoke it — Clint with tongue-oil enough to run a whole fleet of windmills? Or was it that cook at the Lone Star Grub?

No, by God, it was Frailey; and Marratt suddenly remembered how the old doc had used it. They'd been talking about Ryerson and Frailey had advised, "What Wineglass says is same as law in these sandhills — the marshal's his man just as much as Churk Crafkin."

So this bullypuss baiter of defenseless squaws was one of Ryerson's crowd. A hired gun thrower probably. The notion didn't raise the cow king much in Marratt's opinion; it fit snug enough though with the rest he'd learned about him.

Marratt dropped Crafkin's hat and reckoned he'd better cut a shuck toward Usher's before some more of Ryerson's range-roughing maverick makers got wind of him. Next time, like enough, the breaks would be with Wineglass and this gulch wasn't Marratt's idea of the kind of a place a man would want to be trapped in.

He made slow work of getting back through the brush to where he'd left the rented gelding. His gymnastics with Crafkin hadn't helped the convalescing of that bullet track any and his cracked rib was aching like an ulcerated tooth. It wouldn't endure any further sudden bendings but it didn't keep his thinking away from that dratted squaw.

She certainly had Marratt fighting his hat and he admitted it. He couldn't think why he'd gone and stuck his crazy neck out. Some bulls, people claimed, couldn't stand a red rag and maybe he was like that when it came to baiting women — like that poor sap, Don Quixote, who couldn't pass a goddam windmill.

Any kid in three-cornered pants would have known better than to go ramming into a play the girl had patently invited. If she hadn't wanted Crafkin's attentions why had she come there to wait for him?

Why, indeed, Marratt wondered, abruptly remembering some other things. The first time he'd seen her she had been in Beckwith's office. Then he'd found her at that tank. How the hell had she got to this gulch to be waiting for Ryerson's man in the first place?

That had taken some traveling; Churk Crafkin himself hadn't picked any daisies once he'd discovered the supposed Luke on his trail.

Marratt swore irritably. The whole thing was such a damned mixed-up tangle a man couldn't hardly tell straight-up from down. Only one thing looked certain: There was some sort of tie-up between Beckwith, that squaw and Churk Crafkin. There was another — or was it the same? — between Beckwith, Ryerson and Crafkin. And where did Clint Gainor come into this deal?

On the theory of first things first Marratt tried to work it out on the basis of time but was distracted from that when another thought hit him. This conception was so cogent it turned him clear around and sent him back toward the scene of his encounter with Crafkin. He hated bitterly to waste further time that might prove precious but he'd come here for information and even one concrete fact could be a damned sight more valuable than the mess of loose ends he now had hold of. It might turn out to be the key which would put sense into all he'd discovered.

He moved fast as he dared but kept his gun in hand just in case that fellow Crafkin should be up and about again. The girl had gone off with the burly gun fighter's horse. He might be in a mood to do murder if he'd recovered that pistol.

But there was no sign of Crafkin when Marratt came into the clearing. Apparently the guy had found his gun and struck out afoot to get back to ranch headquarters; he wouldn't waste any time and, once he got to Ryerson, they'd have the whole crew out scouring this country.

It was horse tracks Marratt had returned for a look at and when he found them he had his fact. It was the girl, not Crafkin, he'd trailed into this gulch. She hadn't been waiting for Crafkin. He'd been waiting here for her!

It was after ten when Marratt rode into the Usher yard. Moonglow dappled the buildings with silver but Marratt right then had no eye peeled for beauty. He was weary in mind as well as in body and had to just about pry himself out of the saddle; but he was too much a

78

cowman not to care for his horse.

He pulled off the gear and spread the damp blanket where the wind could get at it. He rubbed the gelding down thoroughly with wisps of old straw from the leaky barn and then staked him out where he could fill up on grass. He fetched him a pail of water and finally headed for the house.

That cracked rib was giving him hell in good measure but he forgot all about it when he stepped onto the stoop. In the center of the door there was a fluttering square of paleness that made a sound like flapping paper.

Marratt's bleak eyes narrowed and he stood there several moments before he at last pulled it loose and went inside and eased the door shut. Only then did he strike a match for there was that much caution left in him.

Two lines of block letters had been inscribed with a pencil.

USHER: KEEP RIDING IF YOU
WANT TO KEEP BREATHING

He was still staring at it when he realized he wasn't alone.

Chapter 7

He was tempted — urged by every instinct of self-preservation — to let go of the match and grab for his gun, but common sense kept him motionless. If whoever was watching had wanted to kill him they'd have done so the moment flame had leaped from that matchstick.

He said, "Well?"

"Put that light to a lamp."

"What about the windows?"

"They're all taken care of."

Marratt crossed to the wall and lifted the lamp's chimney. He rubbed the flame across the wick, watched it take hold and flare orange and smoky, and set the glass back on. Only then did he face the sound of the voice to find Gainor eyeing him across a cocked pistol.

The man motioned toward a chair. "Take the load off your feet. We've got some rag-chewin' to do —"

"You put this thing on the door?"

Gainor grinned. "Not me. That was one of your other friends. You know —" his sly eyes brightened with a secret amusement, "you're lucky, at that. Mostly, around here, they just hang up the crepe."

"You're wasting your time," Marratt told him. "You made me your offer and —"

"I made you *an* offer," Gainor remarked pointedly. "Nothin' to keep me from makin' you another."

Marratt said flatly, "I'm not selling this place. And if I was you'd be the last guy I'd consider."

"A man can talk too brash for his own good, my friend."

"Go on — say the rest of it."

"What took you over to the Malicora agency?"

"I don't consider that any of your business."

Anger's roan stain crept through the black of Gainor's whiskers. Resentment plowed through his tone. "You better take another squint at your holecard! You're playin' a wolf's game that's goin' to get rougher an' you're like to hev need of all the help you can get here."

"I'll pick my own help, thank you."

"Why, you goddam fool . . ."

"Yes?"

Gainor got hold of himself with an effort. "Now see here, Luke," he wheedled, "we got too much in common, you an me, to go flyin' at each other like a couple of trollops. Let's chew this over calm-like an see —"

"You talk a lot," Marratt said, "but you don't say anything. What the hell are you holding that gun for?"

Gainor grinned through his tangle of whiskers. "Let's just say for the good o' my soul," he said, chuckling. Then his look turned cunning. "I got a stake in this business myself; I got my back ag'in' the same wall you hev. That should make us compadres if nothin' else would. Ryerson's usin' this place an', one way or another, he means to hev mine. So the natural thing —"

"I don't see it," Marratt said. "I've been given to understand Ryerson's got pretty powerful. If he wants your place why doesn't he grab it?"

"You mean same's he grabbed this one? It ain't quite that simple. Situations are different. I ain't got no ol' man to be killed like Jake Usher; an' I'm still squattin' on mine. I ain't aimin' to skip out."

He let that sink in, his eyes watching Marratt blandly. "Besides," he said abruptly, "he's buildin' a loop for the legislature. He kinda fancies droppin' his butt in the governor's chair an', till Murphey's term's up, he'd prefer to slide around the strong-arm stuff an' let things simmer in the status quo."

"You think that's why someone tried to drygulch me?"

Gainor's hooded eyes widened. But he said coolly enough, "You kin see for yourself he wouldn't want no old scandals bein' dug up around here now. I tell you, Luke, we're in this together an' if you aim to stick it out here you're goin' to need help. You won't get no more warnin's."

"Suppose you come to the point."

Gainor peered at him, frowning. "Well," he said gruffly, "I'd like to hev this spread outright, but if you're bound to hang onto it I'll buy in as pardner. That's fair enough, ain't it?"

Marratt studied him thoughtfully. He guessed perhaps Gainor'd said a bit more than he'd aimed to. If Ryerson didn't want trouble right now there was a fair to middling chance he wouldn't buck too strenuously any move on Marratt's part to rid Usher range of Wineglass cattle. Gainor, he reckoned, would be counting on that. He wasn't exactly figuring to throw his money away.

"But why," Marratt asked, "would you want to buy into it? We could still be allies —"

"You'd be more apt to consider my end of

83

this stick if I had a sizeable stake in your out-fit. There's nothin' wrong with your spread a little money wouldn't cure."

"You keep talking around things. If you want to do business fetch it out in the open. Just what do you propose?"

"A fifty-fifty interest with you continuing to manage the ranch."

"As presumptive owner?"

"That's correct," Gainor grinned. "Because if anything goes wrong I ain't honin' to have Ryerson camped in my hair any more'n he is already — for as long, anyway, as I am able to prevent it. You'll be the big cheese; I'll be your silent pardner."

"And you'll expect me to use the price of your half to stock it?"

"No," Gainor said, "I'll pay my share toward puttin' stock on it."

"What's the amount of your offer for this proposed half interest?"

"Six thousand dollars."

"I'll think it over," Marratt said.

Gainor sidled around him, still with his gun out. At the door, he said, "I'll want your answer tomorrow. It could be damn unfortunate for both of us if Ryerson should discover we're havin' any dealin's. There's a can of white paint in the barn. If the answer's yes, put a coat of it on your chimney."

Marratt was too bone weary after Gainor's departure to think any further about anything. He pulled off Luke's boots and old Jake's gun belt, wedged a chair beneath the knob of the door which had held the warning and dropped exhausted across the couch.

The sun was high when he awoke the next morning. The first thing he did after a hasty splash was to soothe the pangs of his growling stomach. Then, with Jake's artillery once again strapped about him and a fourth steaming cup of black coffee before him, he sat down to some serious thinking.

Though Gainor's talk last night had held a reasonable sound, going over it step by step convinced Marratt it was geared to a pattern reminiscent of that which had fetched the man out to see him that first time. Gainor had an axe he was bent on grinding and was craftily hoping to maneuver the supposed Luke into turning the stone. Gainor wanted the ranch but deep in his scheming was some festering sore that was not to be healed short of Ryerson's death. This was the core of Marratt's impression.

How much of the man's talk had been built from whole cloth was debatable, but the ring of sincerity had marked his voice when he'd declared all he wanted was Usher's signature on a quitclaim. Failing to get it he'd come round with this new deal.

Marratt felt pretty sure if he had signed away the ownership of Usher's grass Ryerson would now be dead and Luke saddled with the killing — the supposed Luke, of course. And even granting as true all of Gainor's talk last night, the net result of teaming up with him would likely still be the same. A dead man at Wineglass and Marratt on the run.

There might be other things mixed into Clint Gainor's thinking which impelled the man to such antigodlin tactics as concealing his horse and coming only after dark; as suggesting Marratt show his choice by painting a chimney and holding a loaded gun on him while offering a partnership. But there wasn't any doubt in Marratt's mind the main goal of Gainor's endeavoring was Ryerson's death.

And what of the girl from Beckwith's office? Where did she fit into what was going on around here?

He cursed the persistence with which his thoughts kept harking back to that brown-eyed squaw. Light complexioned she might be, and pretty as a speckled pup under a red wagon, but she was still a squaw so far as Marratt was concerned. Those black braids told the story, and the quickening suspicion that some of her folks might not have worn mocassins did little to make her more acceptable. She was still a woman, and there was no place for women — red, black, white or yellow — in the plans which had dug Grete Marratt out of Yuma.

He scowled bleakly at the steam curling up off his coffee.

Like it or not, she was going to have to be considered. She was part and parcel of whatever was going on or she would not have slipped her tether to keep a rendezvous with Crafkin. Well . . . *would* she? If that meeting had been simply an affair of the heart would she have been trying to fight Ryerson's understrapper off? What story had she concocted to explain her absence to Beckwith?

Every angle he sought to follow dead-ended against the inescapable fact of Crafkin's presence in that gulch. He'd been waiting there for her and if she hadn't been aware of it why had she gone there?

The only alternative a quarter hour of thinking was able to dredge up was that she'd been heading for Wineglass and Crafkin had intercepted her. How would Crafkin have known this? How could he have guessed at what time she would appear or that she'd have left the regular trail to take so roundabout a route? And, assuming these things could be answered, why would he want to stop her?

It was palpably too far-fetched to be given credence. Was it less far-fetched to assume the government had hired her to take care of Beckwith's paper work? Yet, if she were Beckwith's wife or Beckwith's woman, would a man of the agent's puling character have dared thus to flaunt her in the faces of his underpaid white-collar help?

She didn't make sense no matter what role he gave her and he finally tramped outside to put the gelding under gear.

He was going to someway have to get his hands on a chunk of money. He needed more groceries and owed the doc a bill for those he'd already eaten; and he reckoned his hair had grown out enough now to chance the attentions of a barber. His whiskers, too, could stand a trim and he was anxious to see Frailey though he doubted that he would catch him this late in the day.

As things turned out he didn't even have to hunt. The doc came driving into the yard just as Marratt was lifting his left foot to stirrup.

"Fetched you out some more vittles. How's that side coming along?" he hailed, pulling up. "Better let me have another look at it."

Marratt brushed that aside. "It's getting along well enough. I'm glad you came by though. I want to know what I owe you. There's the wound and the grub and this horse you hired for me. I can't keep piling up expenses —"

"You've got to live, haven't you?"

"I don't have to live off your generosity."

Frailey showed a mild surprise. "Well, we can figure it out, I reckon. What are you going to do? Not thinking of working the Half Circle U, are you?"

Marratt assumed that by that Frailey was referring to the Usher ranch. He said, "Any reason why I shouldn't?"

"I understood you'd been warned to clear out of the country."

"Where'd you hear that?"

"It's all over town."

Marratt's solid lips twisted. His big shoulders stirred restively. "If I'd been figuring to leave I wouldn't have come back in the first place. I can't do anything without money — any chance of the Casa Grande bank putting up some?"

Frailey shook his head. "Phelps is in too thick with Ryerson." He considered Marratt narrowly a couple of moments. "You've stayed away too long. Why start something you know will be bound to end in bloodshed?"

"I'm not looking for a fight or aiming to tear any scars off old wounds but —"

"You won't be able to help yourself. If you

stay there'll be trouble — don't that damned warning prove it?"

"I'm staying," Marratt said with his jaws tightening grimly. "What do you know about a fellow that calls himself Clint Gainor?"

Frailey said without expression, "He owns the Boxed Triangle. A not too-important spread bordering Wineglass on the west." He sat watching Marratt for a couple of heart-beats. "Well, let's get this grub put away," he said, getting out of the buggy. "Your dad left a will with myself as administrator. Now that you've returned we can put it through pro-bate; I've been keeping the back taxes paid up for you. There's about $3500 cash, banked in Chandler. You won't be able to draw on that yet but I can let you have a couple of hundred if you'd like."

Marratt said stiffly, "If it wouldn't inconvenience you I'd be glad of the difference be-tween that and what I owe you."

After they'd come back from packing in the groceries Frailey said, "I suppose you'd like it right away? We'll have to go to town then. I ought to be getting back anyway. Hitch your horse on behind and ride up here with me."

"No point rubbing some of the smell off on you."

"Nonsense!" Frailey snapped. "I may not

perhaps be able to prevent your making a fool of yourself, but —"

"I'll ride the horse," Marratt said, and climbed on him.

It wasn't that he didn't like Doc, because he did; but there was no use compromising the old man more than he had to. And if trouble came up he wanted to be in a position to get hold of his gun.

Also there was this matter of pride. He reckoned he owed something to the man whose name and clothes he was wearing. He didn't want folks who might see them to say he'd come into Bella Loma trying to hide behind Frailey.

He thought of Clint Gainor bellied down someplace waiting for him to daub white paint on a chimney. Recalling the way the man had kept that gun on him he remembered the odd expression he had several times trapped in the fellow's too-bright eyes. It were as though the joker had been steeling himself to the unburdening of something he couldn't cut loose of; every time he'd get that look he'd kind of take hold of his gun a little tighter.

The doc was pulling up before Danvers' General Store. Reining his gelding over to the tie rack Marratt got down and joined Frailey on the porch. "We'll step in here," the latter said quietly. "I'll get a check cashed and give you that money —"

"Just the difference," Marratt nodded, "between what you've offered and what I already owe you. Two hundred is all I can afford to be in debt."

As they were about to move inside, a deeply bronzed goddess in starched gingham, arms stacked with bundles and black hair piled against the flash of a Spanish comb, twisted gracefully through the door with a quick smile as her eyes met Frailey's.

The doctor removed his hat. "Naome," he said, "I would like for you to meet Luke Usher. Luke, this is Clem Ryerson's daughter."

Marratt started, features frozen, stopping dead in his tracks. It was the willowy 'squaw' he had rescued from Crafkin — the girl of the tank and Beckwith's office!

Chapter 8

Churk Crafkin, by the time he came limping into Wineglass headquarters, was in the sod-pawing mood of an affronted bull moose. He went storming through the house banging doors like a twister and if he'd gotten his hands on Naome right then there'd have been a sure understanding of who was boss around here. He didn't find her, of course, because she'd fled to Bella Loma.

Grinding his teeth he came back into the yard and that was when he noticed the lamplit window of his shanty. Highboned cheeks still stiff with anger, he veered away from the course that would have taken him to the bunkhouse. He'd told the crew more than once to stay out of his diggings and if he found one of them in there now he was minded to break the snoopy bastard's neck.

He came into the place like a wet-footed cat and the hooded look of his eyes turned black as obsidian when he observed the gaunt shape which came out of his rocker. "What the hell," he said roughly, "are you doin' here, Beckwith?"

Beckwith quailed from his look, thrust a hand out placatingly. "I — know you told me never to come here," he gulped, "but something terrible has happened! Where is Mr. Ryerson?"

"What do you want with Ryerson?"

"I've got to see him right —"

"You *can't* see him. He's off on one of his trips, pullin' strings to get that appointment. Now quit that damn shakin' and tell me what's got your bowels in an uproar."

"It's those wretched Usher cattle!" Beckwith blurted. "Some fellow came into my office this mor—"

"Hold it," growled Crafkin, and swung around and very carefully closed the door. Then he went to the windows and pulled both shades. When he came back his cheeks were like slabs of granite. "Now let's have it," he said, "and keep your goddam voice down."

The perspiring agent, with many lip-chewing pauses, nervously sketched in the salient features of Marratt's visit while Crafkin's eyes turned blacker and blacker. With the skin stretched tight across the jut of his cheekbones Crafkin finally asked, "You see Naome today?"

"Naome?" Beckwith stared at him stupidly.

"All right," Crafkin growled. "What'd this guy look like?"

"The fellow was obviously Usher —"

"You never saw Usher; he left before you come here —"

"But I told you —"

"Never mind what you told me. Describe him."

Beckwith stammeringly did so and the Wineglass ramrod reluctantly nodded. "It was him, right enough," he said, as though to himself, "but what I can't understand is —"

"You haven't heard the worst of it. I'd been outside talking with a couple of Indians. When I came in he was already there — in my office, I mean. In a chair," Beckwith said, swallowing hard, "by the desk. I hadn't any reason right then to be suspicious — like you said, I'd never met up with either of the Ushers. And I was — I'll admit it — pretty shaken up by the time he'd gone stamping out of there. Coming at me that way right out of the blue . . . but —"

"For Chrissake," Crafkin snarled, "get on with it!"

Beckwith mopped his face. "After — after I'd got my mind squared around to it, I got to thinking about those cancelled checks —"

"You goddam fool! Mean to say you been keepin' —"

"Yes. Of course." A faint surprise flittered through Beckwith's frightened stare. "Naturally, I've been keeping them — it would have looked rather odd, don't you think, if I hadn't? — I had them filed by date with all the rest of our beef checks —"

"And now they're gone?"

Beckwith licked his parched lips, "I can't find them."

Ryerson's range boss glared. He hulked above Beckwith like an outraged orangoutang; but, strangely enough, he didn't strike him, didn't curse.

"All right," he said at last. "I'll take care of this. Clear out of here now and keep your mouth shut."

Crafkin, as soon as Beckwith had gone, went back to the house with pulses racing. Here, if he could just get his hands on them, was the best possible weapon he could get for his purpose. That bungled attempt he'd made to compromise Naome — even had it been successful — would never have given him one-tenth the shocking power he'd be able to wring from those cancelled checks.

Not for an instant did he believe Luke had gotten them — it was that damned brat of

Ryerson's. She'd been a heap too elaborate in her departure this morning, babbling to cookie how she was figuring to visit that sick nester woman over on Breakneck Creek, then dawdling around until the crew had been dispatched before setting off in that outlandish getup.

If she'd been any kin of his, Crafkin would have taken a rope's end to her before he'd have let her flaunt her old man's shame all over the goddam cactus. But it wasn't her costume which had sharpened his suspicions. Always — ever since she had been grown enough to get into them — she'd taken a bastardly delight larruping around in them trifling gewgaws. That crap had been her mother's and, like her blank-faced Injun stubbornness, had become familiar enough by this time to go unnoticed. It was her un-Injunlike chatter, her shining up to the cook, which had caught at Crafkin's attention. He had let her get a couple of hours' start, then had tracked her long enough to make sure she'd been bound for Beckwith's.

He had angrily supposed she was having an affair with the agent and it was this which, having watched for her return, had decided him not to wait any longer and launched the savage coup brought to naught by that dog of an Usher.

Too long and much too carefully had Crafkin been at pains to insure this big spread's future to be cheated of his intention at this late date. All through the years — even before that day at the Half Circle U — he'd been working to bring about Ryerson's sudden death or downfall in such fashion as would give himself complete control of Wineglass — if not outright possession. By patient and crafty maneuvering he had made Clem Ryerson into a feared and hated cattle king; it was Crafkin, not Ryerson, who had made Wineglass all-powerful. It was a tribute to the ramrod's genius that not even Ryerson suspected this.

But patience was a thing any man could get fed up with and Usher's return had badly jolted Crafkin; he couldn't understand how he had gone so astray in his judgment.

Ryerson had been out of town at the time, away on this string-pulling trip he'd arranged for him; the range boss, dangerously rattled, had attempted to gun Usher down from ambush. Poor light and distance had played hob with his marksmanship, but he had certainly expected Usher to panic. Instead of hauling his freight as he had that other time, the crazy fool had moved into his abandoned ranch house and gone snooping around that chiseling agent's office.

Crafkin's black orbs winnowed down to glittering slits every time he recalled facing Usher in that gulch; but those cancelled checks were the important things right now. The problem of Usher and where he'd gotten such courage could wait, like Naome, till he got hold of those three-by-eight pieces of paper. Once those were in his hands he'd have a real whip to work with; his mind would be unfettered to put the screws on all of them.

Through the rage churning through him came one lancing streak of caution that swung him completely around on the porch and sent his bull voice over the yard. "Tularosa!"

Into the glow of the lamp he'd left burning came a bony breed with forward-hunched shoulders who was clad in a dirty pair of cotton *pantalones* and a dirtier cotton shirt gaping open to his navel. A club foot gave him a crablike motion which was no more repulsive than the rabbit's pink eyes in the pockmarked face upturned to await Crafkin's orders.

"Mount the crew and put them to combing the flats and gulches for sign of Luke Usher — I run onto him down by Snake Canyon shining up to Naome. He's probably dug for the tules but tell 'em to make sure. Then come back here and sit on this porch till I call you."

He didn't wait for an answer but, turning, tramped inside, picking up the lamp and going into the girl's bedroom. He personally hired every man in this outfit, inconspicuously replacing those who'd been on the place when he had come here to manage it so that Ryerson could spend more time prospecting around for that goldmine he'd used to be hipped on. But Tularosa was the only one he put any trust in. Marihuana was the key to the warped and twisted gunman; Crafkin kept the halfwit in smoking and got in turn a doglike devotion which he'd found extremely useful on more than one occasion. He had sometimes toyed with the thought of using him on Ryerson, and he might even yet if he couldn't hit on anything better.

Now for those checks!

First he examined the flooring. When he'd convinced himself there were no loose boards he started on the bed, running every inch of the quilt through careful fingers before dropping it into a heap on the floor. Kicking it out of his way he stripped off the sheets and, with his knife, got to work on the mattress.

He wasn't worried about her squawking. She had too much Injun to go tattling to Ryerson.

While he worked his thoughts slipped back seventeen years and he was remembering the towering rage he'd been in when Ryerson, lank and drawn and looking bleached as a cadaver, had come back from one of his mine-hunting trips with the goddam squaw who had been Naome's mother. She had found him delirious and dying from snakebite at the edge of a waterhole and nursed him back to health.

She'd been a good-looking wench — even Crafkin had been willing to concede that much — and he could have understood Ryerson keeping her around — at least for a little while. But marrying her! And publicly!

He had come almighty near throwing up the job until he'd sensed the effect it was having on Ryerson's neighbors. Then the big idea had hit him. If Ryerson was dope enough to get hitched up to a redskinned squaw he might be fool enough to let Churk Crafkin take this spread away from him.

It was worth a little thought and he had given it plenty. It was after the squaw had found Ryerson a papoose that Crafkin decided he had better get rid of her. A girl he could handle; he didn't want no fool boys.

He didn't have Tularosa on the payroll in those days and there was no hemlock handy, so he'd introduced a handful of chopped-up oleander into the mustard greens she'd been boiling one day while Ryerson was over to the county seat. It hadn't worked quite as rapid as he had reckoned it would but it had finally taken care of her in spite of old Frailey's efforts.

He'd thought for awhile the boss would go off his rocker, and he had been kind of worried because he hadn't been ready to discard Ryerson then; he'd needed a front for the steals he'd been planning.

But it had worked out all right because the chump had gone off on a mine-hunting bender, clean out of this world, away back of beyond. Months he'd been gone, trying to turn up that bonanza he had used to talk so much about. He hadn't ever found it but he'd kept right on hunting, along the border, deep into the Saucedas — once he'd even been sighted as far north as Humboldt, and another time over along the Santa Maria River, west of Skull Valley. He was a traveling fool if Churk had ever seen one.

Of course he was back off and on and every once in a while he'd be seen around long enough to give folks the notion he was passing out the orders. Crafkin managed with considerable ingenuity to let Ryerson have all the credit for his skullduggery. He always publicly regretted the things he was forced to do; and whenever he was about to clamp down on some outfit he would always fetch Clem Ryerson around beforehand, adroitly fostering the impression he was there himself only because the cattle king had ordered him to be.

He remembered the first time Ryerson had taken Naome with him. She hadn't been over three or four at the time but "She's got to learn self-reliance," the boss had explained. "Some day she's going to be the owner of this spread and I aim for her to know what the score is when she gets it. When she's older you can teach her all you know about the cow business. She's got some hard knocks ahead of her, people bein' what they are. She can best be got ready to meet them by a thorough acquaintance with nature."

It had been evident to Crafkin right then he had a screw loose. It had been evident before but, if further proof were needed, that kind of talk supplied it. The guy was loco as a hootowl. When she'd fallen off her horse he'd picked her up and set her on again, never paying no more attention to her tears than Crafkin would have paid to a horned toad. When they'd rode off into the shimmering desert he had reckoned he'd seen the last of her and didn't much care one way or the other.

It was when she was nine and beginning to bud out that he'd finally made up his mind he would marry her as the easiest way of making sure he got Wineglass. Strangely enough she had never taken to him, always meeting cold-eyed his most artful advances. Two years ago he'd quit bothering his head with her, telling himself that when the sign was right she would be damned glad to hitch up with him.

He'd have had her dead to rights today if that dog of an Usher hadn't come riding into it.

Usher's presence had stimulated one idea though. He would see that folks were reminded of the threats Luke had made after old Jake's killing. Then, if Ryerson turned up with a hole through his skull, this country'd have no trouble knowing where to place the blame.

He had mattress stuffing strewn all over the floor and still no sign of those goddam checks. He pulled her clothes off their hooks and began emptying drawers. He tore the pillows apart. He just about turned the place upside down before at last he faced the fact she must have taken the checks with her.

He dropped the knife back into his boot and slammed the door shut behind him. His eyes were like agate as he headed for the porch. There was just one place she could reasonably have gone. Ryerson kept a year-around room at the Buffalo Bull, Bella Loma's only rooming house with any pretentions to grandeur. That was where he would find her.

"Get your horse," he told Tularosa, "I've an idea Miss Naome will be needing your attentions."

Marratt was still staring, still locked tight in the grip of his astonishment, when the girl said, "How do you do?"

Her contralto voice was cool as fresh spring water. Her eyes behind black lashes were as gravely polite and impersonal as though she were considering an utter stranger. And yet he sensed behind this show of mild interest an on-guard sort of feeling that made him say perversely, "Haven't I come across you someplace before, Miss Ryerson?"

Her eyes regarded his with a not too-interested curiosity, "I can't seem to recall the occasion. Perhaps you have me mixed up with some other girl you've met during the course of your extended travels."

He felt a stir of admiration for the quick-thinking smoothness with which she'd turned the talk back on him. He guessed she must have done a bit of traveling herself to have acquired such a nonchalant facility with words.

As though divining his thought, she said smiling, "I've never been outside Arizona, Mr. Usher, and all the schooling I've had I got from my dad during trips we used to take when we were hunting the foot of the rainbow. Of course," she added reflectively, "I've done a little reading . . . Walter Scott, some Dickens and Thackeray."

Marratt reckoned to know when he was being made fun of. "And do you add swimming, Miss Ryerson, to your other accomplishments?"

Her eyes returned his look demurely. "A girl doesn't have many chances around here —"

"I suppose working for one's living does take up a deal of one's time?"

"She doesn't work," Frailey said, looking curiously from one to the other of them.

"Then what was she doing at the Malicora Agency, got up like an Indian, when I saw her yesterday morning?"

Naome laughed. "I'm afraid Mr. Usher's a rather imaginative person," she told Frailey. "And now, if you'll excuse me, I think I'd better go see if Dad came in on the stage."

"I'll go with you," Marratt said quickly. "I've been meaning to have a —"

"Daddy!" the girl cried; and Marratt swung round as a spare sunbronzed man with white hair and blue store clothes stepped onto the porch and came toward them. Tired eyes smiled at Naome and then looked closely at Marratt. "How are you, Usher?" he said quietly, and reached out a hand.

Frailey slanched a nervous glance at Usher's belted gun; but Marratt never noticed.

His stare leaped from the three fingers of that outstretched hand to the uptilted nose and jagged track of a knife scar lividly marking Ryerson's left temple.

Naome screamed.

Chapter 9

Thirty years of patching bones and stitching hides for the folks who ranched the Bella Loma country had given Doc Frailey a considerable insight into the foibles and follies of a matured humanity. He had come to believe he could pretty well predict how the most of them would react to any given set of circumstances; yet the returned Luke Usher was continually amazing him, so unlike was the man to Frailey's preconceived notions.

He remembered Luke well as a gawky lad of sixteen, loud of mouth, always complaining and given to violent rages when things didn't go the way his mind was bent on having them. Clumsy as a colt and never knowing what to do with his hands when they weren't wrapped about some firearm, he'd been considerably taken up with his own importance and over-ready to resent the least infringement of his imagined due. Half Circle U had been the most prosperous spread at this end of the cactus and Luke had been very determined folks should keep that fact well in mind.

And, mostly, they had while in Luke Usher's presence; because, in addition to his irascible temper, he was known far and wide as a red striped whizzer when it came to putting a belt gun in action. He was also known for his love of the bottle, and this combination was not of a kind many married men cared to shove out their jaws at. They'd been made too aware of Luke's homicidal tendencies to cherish any illusions regarding their own rights and privileges.

Thus had talk roundabout been stirred to a fever heat when, after Jake's killing and Luke's subsequent brags, the local champion of six-shooter justice had cravenly tucked tail and proceeded to roll his twine. Doc Frailey, however, had not been noticeably surprised, his friendship with Jake having privately convinced him Luke's bark had been infinitely more lethal than his bite.

He had always been prepared to concede the boy dangerous, but mainly where circumstances were arranged to his advantage. With better opportunity than most to observe him Frailey had personally considered Usher's son to be a bully battening on a gratuitous rep he hadn't any right to. He had made his brags that night while drunk and obviously forgetful of the man who didn't have to brag — Churk Crafkin, Ryerson's range boss.

An outlander hired two years before to ramrod Wineglass, Churk Crafkin was believed to hail from Texas where, it was clandestinely rumored, he'd gut-shot several men in a feud before seeking greener pastures to preserve his continued health. According to the way Frailey'd viewed the matter Luke, when he had got sufficiently sober to recall the frozen-faced Texican, had made up his mind in a hurry which part of valor was like to return the greatest dividends. He had flown the coop exactly as the doctor would have expected him to.

Frailey *had* been surprised to stumble onto Luke in the rain that night he had encountered him in the road out front of the old Usher ranch house. He'd thought at first his eyes had been playing him tricks, that the fancied resemblance to the blustering Luke was simply the result of imagination on proximity. But when he'd carried him inside and got him stripped beneath Jake's picture their alikeness had been too apparent for him to entertain further doubt.

Incredible as it might appear to him, and contrary to all his most cherished predictions, Luke had come back to the obligations he'd run out on. Or, at least, he'd come back. And characteristically broke.

It had not astonished Frailey to discover he'd been shot, things being the way they were, but he'd been definitely astonished when Luke had failed to enlarge on the subject, and even more so when, during their first exchange of words, he'd volunteered no explanation. This wasn't much like the Luke Doc remembered.

Nor was his voice, nor his mannerisms, nor the direct challenging way in which those inscrutable eyes regarded you. Beyond the matter of looks there was practically nothing discernible about the fellow which reminded Frailey of the Luke he had known in the old days — the loud-mouthed Luke who had pulled his freight after telling the town what he would do to Clem Ryerson.

Frailey'd never believed in leopards changing their spots, but he hadn't believed Luke would come back, either, so perhaps after all he'd been wrong about leopards. After ten days of Usher he'd begun to believe so and to even look forward to having the man around again. He'd begun to find in Luke traits he'd known in his father and these in turn had engendered hopes he might be able to talk Luke out of any notions he might have of kicking sleeping dogs awake.

111

Whatever the man had in mind regarding Wineglass, it was plainly no concern of Frailey's. Wineglass was able to look out for itself. The big trouble with that line of reasoning was that it presupposed the outfit and its owner to be synonymous — a probability the doctor wasn't ready to accept. He knew Ryerson's neighbors had never questioned this assumption but the doctor wasn't the sort to let popular beliefs lead astray his own conclusions. He was still far from satisfied Ryerson fit the local conception.

Frailey had fetched Naome into this world and, because of her mixed blood, had done considerable thinking about her, carefully watching the result of Ryerson's influence. She'd been much away on long trips with her father and had herself told the doctor a great deal about these without realizing she was doing so. It had been good medicine, he thought.

Under Ryerson's guidance she had learned about life from nature, from the observance of birds and animals and the study of their ways with each other; a hard school, perhaps but thorough. Nor had the man neglected the more formal aspects of her education; he had taught her to read and write along with self-reliance and grounded her in the more useful other things she might have learned had he sent her away to school.

Frailey felt pretty sure he understood why Ryerson hadn't.

The girl's thinking was direct and wholesome, no vicious misconceptions or evil gossip had unbalanced it. Her mind was clean, graceful and attractive as her body; and for these things the old man respected Ryerson.

Whether or not the rancher had killed Jake Usher — as Luke had proclaimed — he had no means of knowing, but he did not believe the man deliberately had planned to put his neighbors out of business for the benefit of Wineglass; that kind of man would never have established the rapport Ryerson enjoyed with Naome.

The doctor could not brush away the fact that several smaller outfits had been absorbed into Ryerson's holdings; but a lot might depend on how much rope he'd given his ramrod. On how much of the rancher's authority the man had taken on himself.

Clem Ryerson was Naome's father and what hurt Ryerson was bound also to hurt Ryerson's daughter. In direct proportion to the tie between them.

This was the fact which had influenced Frailey's hope that he might steer Luke away from any further trouble with Wineglass. And, knowing from past experience how

stubborn an Usher could be, he had welcomed this chance of introducing Luke to
Naome.

He'd been totally unprepared for the turn
Luke's talk had taken. He'd been a lot more
disconcerted than the girl appeared to be but
he had glimpsed one thing which had given
him cause for renewed hope. Whether or not
he yet realized it the girl's appeal had got under Luke's hide pretty deeply. Given a little
time such magic might well work wonders.

It was therefore with considerable misgiv-
ings that Frailey watched Clem Ryerson
round the store's north corner and step onto
the porch. The rancher's glance found them
instantly. The doctor stood with caught
breath as Ryerson came up to them and,
putting out his hand, said quietly, "How are
you, Usher?"

It was not the remark or manner of a man
laboring under a guilty conscience but the
doctor could not help looking nervously at the
belted gun riding Usher's right thigh. It was
while he was looking that Naome screamed.

Frailey's glance jerked up. The look in
Luke's face made his guts turn cold and
crawl. He could not blame the girl for crying
out or for the frantic way she'd flung herself,
arms spread, between that vision and her father.

Ryerson's own cheeks were gray but his eyes never wavered. He said, "Keep out of this, Naome," and put her gently aside. "If you've come back," he told Luke, "to wind up any unfinished business, don't let a child's hysteria stand in your way."

Frailey's jaws ached with strain. He could see and he could hear but he was powerless to move. The words he would have spoken were all piled up and clogged in his throat. He was like a man in the path of a rampaging cyclone, immobilized by his grasp of impending disaster.

For the space of ten heartbeats there was no sound whatever. Then, immeasurably, so slightly as only to be sensed rather than seen, the frozen stillness of Usher's stance became again imbued with breathing. The killer look leached out of his stare and he stepped back half a pace to say with bitter clarity: "Next time your tracks cross mine have a gun on you."

He swung round on his heel and stepped off the porch.

Chapter 10

It was late, close to one, when Tularosa reached town. The only lights still showing came with a lemon effulgence through the dust-grimed windows of the Red Horse Bar. He didn't care about that; light, at this stage, not being essential to his purpose. He had been given by Crafkin, before taking off, just enough of his favorite poison to see him through his present chore and fetch him back for refueling.

Crafkin had told him where to find the girl and what manner of things he was to look for in the event she refused to hand them over. Four little pieces of pale green paper measuring three-by-eight with writing and numbers on them.

He pulled up his horse and scrabbled a hand across his bristled face. The lemon glow from the Red Horse Bar looked a million miles away and about as fat as the top of a pin's head. He felt unutterably lonely but he

116

wasn't shaking and he knew what he was here for. The black haired girl had Churk's little green papers and when he fetched them home he would get another smoke.

He sat his saddle awhile pleasantly dreaming about it when, with a renewed depression brought about by his aloneness, he was reminded of what that smoke depended on and his eyes raked the shadows with a mounting fright. He knew from Crafkin where to find the girl but he couldn't think where he was in relation to it.

He kicked the horse into movement that seemed slow as a snail's pace. The Buffalo Bull, Churk Crafkin had said. First room off the right of the second floor hall.

He found the place finally, drenched with sweat. He got out of the saddle and pulled the horse around back where he tied it in the gloom of an ancient pepper tree. Then he retraced his steps to the front and went in. Churk had said, "Be quiet about it," and when he found the banister he went up the stairs with all the stealth of a spider.

First door on the right.

The place was darker than a wolf den but his clammy fingers felt their way across the door till they closed on the smooth metallic feel of the knob and cautiously turned until it would go no farther. His heart was thumping like the pounding of a stamp mill but he pushed infinitesimally and knew it wasn't locked. Lifting up on the knob then to circumvent squeaks he edged it slowly open till he could slip inside after which he quietly edged it shut.

The room was totally black. But night's coolness came from an opened window and gradually his eyes made out the shape of the bed.

He stood perfectly still for a long while remembering the black haired girl in a hundred poses. He swallowed uncomfortably and licked his cracked lips. He dilated his nostrils trying to catch the clean smell of her and lewdly imagined how she'd look without clothes on. If she didn't tell him right away about those papers he'd find out.

Excited by the prospect he moved toward the bed warily. A groping hand touched the near edge and with the stealth of a stalking cat he was crouched at its head, breathing raggedly. Swiftly bending then, cracked lips pulled back from his stumps of teeth, he put out his left, nervously feeling for her body while his spraddle-fingered right, poised hawklike, hung ready to be clapped across her mouth if she sought to holla.

But that creeping left hand couldn't find her.

With a frustrated snarl he raked both hands

across the bed savagely, still not finding her. But she *had* to be in this room — Churk had said she was!

She must be hiding!

Voice turned wheedling, he called to her softly, cunningly coaxing her to show herself quickly lest she be done out of this treasure he had fetched her. When it seemed these blandishments were going to be ignored he crawled under the bed, thrashing about like a snake with its head off. He went into the closet but she wasn't there, either.

He sank onto the bed, hardly able to believe it. His frantic stare raked the intolerable blackness and he got down on all fours, creeping twice around the walls, muttering cajoleries and curses. He got up, soaked with sweat, and thrust his head out the window. A terrible sense of isolation oppressed him and he commenced to shake, feeling hot and cold together. He shook worse when he thought of going back empty-handed.

What he needed was a smoke — but there would be no more smokes without he got Churk those papers.

The girl must have holed up someplace else for the night. It was too frilling early to make a hunt for her now — be quiet, Churk had said. He whimpered like a dog that has been forced to sleep outside.

Because he didn't know what else to do he remained where he was until the sun's yellow disc proclaimed another day was starting, then he crouched behind the window, anchoring his attention on the Lone Star Grub. At eight fifteen this vigil was rewarded when he saw the black haired girl go through the warped screen of its door.

Ten minutes later he was sitting his horse by the tie rack fronting the general store, a gaunt ungainly shape with hunched shoulders. His lips peeled back in bitter outrage when the girl left the hash house with Ives Hanna, the marshal.

He climbed off his horse and went into the store, watched them stand awhile, talking, through the dust-grimed window. He commenced shaking again and, when a clerk stepped over to see what he wanted, the look he gave the fellow would have withered a white oak post. The man scuttled away but the damage was done. Naome had vanished.

He limped outside and got aboard his horse and rode it scowlingly over to Hamp Isham's corral. The girl's bay mare was inside the enclosure, eating hay off the ground with the other nags.

He left his gelding there, telling Isham to feed it, and set off in his crablike motion up the shady side of the street. He loitered across

120

from the marshal's office till he made sure the girl wasn't in there. Something warned him not to ask around for the girl. He finally went and hunkered down outside the blacksmith shop in the shade of a gnarled mesquite, white-ringed stare unswervingly fixed on the mare Ryerson's daughter had left in Isham's corral. When she was minded to leave she would come for it, and when she came for it he meant to be ready.

Marratt, the jingle and scrape of his big-roweled spurs sounding loud in the stillness, stepped off the store's porch and swung into the saddle.

He sat woodenly a moment, hung up in his thoughts, the savage impulse he'd mastered still brightly reflected in the unseeing look he flung over the street. Then he pulled his big shoulders together and sent the hired gelding quartering over the dust on a tangent that would fetch him past Isham's corral. He never noticed the shape squatted by the smith's wall, nor saw how men's heads turned to follow his progress.

He reined in by the twenty-foot mound of baled hay stacked windbreak fashion to the right of the enclosure. Isham, quitting a conversation with one of his helpers, came over. "How'd you find him, Mr. Usher?"

He meant, of course, the horse; and Marratt said after a moment, "He's got plenty of speed but I'd like to get something with a little more bottom and I'm going to tell you right now I haven't got any cash. If you want to make me a deal I'd like that gotch-eared gray yonder. What do you want for him?"

Isham looked at the horse. It was a big raw-boned stallion he had paid too much for considering its temperament and the amount of use he had for it. He told Marratt so. He said, "I'll have to get a hundred dollars for that hide. What bank was you figurin' to give me a check on?"

Marratt hadn't been figuring to give him any check but now he turned the thought over. He still had fifteen thousand in the bank at Prescott. If he drew on that money the law would probably hear of it but he might have ten days before the check could be cleared and traced to Bella Loma. Ten days, with Clagg's partner right here, should give him all the time he would have any need for.

But as he was opening his mouth to name the bank's title and address he suddenly realized the folly of handing Isham any check that didn't carry Usher's signature. In the first place the corral man probably wouldn't take it and, if he did, there'd be talk.

Marratt said, "I was aiming to ask you to

wait a couple days till I can get hold of some cash."

"I guess that will be all right, Mr. Usher. We all know you around here — ain't like as if you was a stranger. You want to use the gear you've got on that geldin'?"

"If you don't mind," Marratt said, and stepped across to a pen that was holding some she stuff. This was not so idle a move as he managed to make it appear. He waved one of the animals around a few paces, admiring its action, covertly noting the comparative size of its tracks. And all the while one part of his mind was still exploring the possibilities of cashing a check.

He needed money — and might be needing it worse before he wound up his score with Clagg's partner. He'd have had his show-down with the skunk right then except for the conditions under which he had met him. When he gunned Clem Ryerson he wanted the man to know why he was being cut down and he couldn't very well state the facts in front of Naome. This was how his mind tried to rationalize the matter but something beyond his mind stood off and jeered at such paltry subterfuge; he wouldn't let himself examine it closer. He had dug his way out of Yuma to kill Clagg's partner and he wasn't about to let anything stop him.

That fifteen thousand was no good to him in Prescott. He couldn't afford to put his name on a check in a region where everyone knew him as Usher. He couldn't do it in Casa Grande but he thought, if he could make the trip quick enough, he might risk going to Ajo or Chandler and, closing out that account, there open a new one under the name of Luke Usher. There'd be plenty of risk but the most of it, he thought, would be wrapped up in the time element, the margin he'd have after passing the check before it could be traced back to him.

Ajo would seem to be the best place to chance it, being the only large town in that end of the Territory. Two horses with plenty of bottom, used in relay, should get him there and back in under twenty-four hours. The thing to do now was cancel the proposed loan and get a blank check from Frailey. Signed by Marratt and made out to Usher, he could. . . .

He said, "What are you asking for this snip-nosed bay?"

"Not mine to sell." Isham shrugged. "That mare belongs to Ryerson's daughter. You want I should throw this hull on that gray?"

"I think," Marratt nodded, "if you're willing to trust me I'd like to have that apron-faced roan yonder also."

Ten minutes later, riding the one and leading the other, he was on his way out of town, headed for Usher's Half Circle U. Not having noticed the squatted shape by the smithy he had no reason for missing it now. The bay mare he'd just seen in the pen at Isham's convinced him that Naome, if she hadn't lied outright, had made a mighty good stab at confusing the issue; for the bay was the same he'd seen hitched outside Beckwith's, the same whose tracked sign had led him to Crafkin. Regardless of the cause or true significance of what he had witnessed, the fact remained that he had found Ryerson's daughter with the fellow, and if it wasn't by her choice then how could it have happened? Why had she been to the agency? Why had she pretended to be working in Beckwith's office and what were those slips —

Marratt suddenly swore. Of course! Those were the checks paid out by Beckwith for the vanished Usher cattle!

He'd been a fool not to realize it sooner.

The first chance she'd got, after learning Luke was back in this country, she'd gone after those checks and gotten away with them. If more proof were needed of Ryerson's involvement than he'd already pried out of Beckwith, she had certainly given it to him. For she would never have taken them without —

125

"That's right, Usher; glad to see you actin' sensible. Just stop right there an' watch those hands if you don't want to catch a blue whistler," Gainor said, edging out of the brush on a mouse-colored dun, a leveled rifle resting lightly across the pommel of his saddle. "You're a kinda hard man to do business with."

"I've decided," Marratt said, "to play a lone hand —"

"What you've decided ain't the point," said Gainor, brushing that aside. "I'm all done with fiddlin' around. You had your chance an' passed it up, so now I'm tellin' you the way it's goin' to be around here. You'll put your name to a paper givin' me — an I said *givin'* — a full half interest in the Half Circle U. As of right now."

"I guess not."

"Then guess again. Furthermore you'll stock it an' hire a crew out of your own pocket, an' you'll get busy right away pushin' Ryerson's cattle out of there."

"You been too long in the sun —"

"I expect," Gainor said, "it's about time I was refreshin' your mem'ry." He gave him a prolonged scrutiny, obviously savoring the situation. "Why do you suppose —"

"You talk too much. Make your point," Marratt told him, "or get out of the way."

A sudden rage seized Gainor and for a moment his eyes showed a blazing malevolence. "You've treated me like dirt for the last time, you bastard! From here on out the shoe'll be on the other foot —"

"You got to make a speech every time you open your trap?"

"That's all right — I kin make your epitaph too, boy. I ain't forgot how you come runnin' around that house with a pistol right after Jake was killed! It was you, not Ryerson, that murdered your ol' man — an' you'll do what I tell you or I'll see you hung for it!"

Chapter 11

After Ryerson left for the ranch with her bundles Naome'd hurried back to Smith's Rooms and hastily changed into her buckskin and squaw boots. She'd wanted mightily to go with her father but hadn't yet found a safe place for those checks so had put him off with the pretended need of visiting that nester's wife out on Breakneck. She'd felt a little uncomfortable about deceiving him, but disliked even more the thought of telling him the truth.

She was sure it had never occurred to him that his range boss could be unfaithful. Her dad in so many ways was like a little boy, living in an imagined world of his own, seeing nothing but good in the people around him, closing his eyes to ugliness and greed. This was weakness, of course, but it was beautiful and she had never been able to bring herself to point out the snake in his garden of Eden.

She had recognized this for weakness, too,

but by using her eyes and her ears she had come to have a pretty bleak conception of their ramrod's real character. She'd unearthed those old rumors concerning why he'd left Texas and had recently talked with a freighter who had known him at Tombstone where Crafkin for awhile had been connected with the Clantons. "That feller's plumb cultus," this old-timer had told her, "an' if he's prowlin' this country I don't want no part of it."

That had started her wondering about the killing of Jake Usher and she'd got hold of the remarks Luke had made while he was drunk, and the story of how he had afterwards vanished — some seemed of the opinion old Jake's son had been bushwhacked.

She knew Wineglass had been using the Usher range for years and that her father and his range boss very seldom discussed ranch business, Ryerson seeming content to leave the spread's management almost entirely in Crafkin's hands. She'd once taxed him with this and he'd said with a laugh, "Naome, honey, that's what I hired the man for, to take all that stuff off my shoulders. Churk's doing all right, don't bother your head with it. He couldn't do better if the place were his own."

He couldn't indeed, she'd thought grimly when, appalled, she had discovered how many smaller spreads had gone into it. She began to notice little things which had escaped her attention before, began to have some understanding of many things which had previously puzzled her such as the attitude of other people's relations with the ranch and with her father. People looked on him as a range hog, on the outfit as though it were some kind of monstrous octopus.

Gradually, insidiously, the notion took hold of her that whenever her dad chanced to visit some other man's holding, this was taken by their neighbors to indicate the approaching end of that spread's independence. And, to her horror, she'd suddenly realized that invariably it had. Within a few weeks or months that place became a part of Wineglass.

With apprehensions mounting Naome had sought to find out whether, previous to old Jake's killing, her father had visited Half Circle U. She found that he had. With Churk Crafkin. She did not know they'd been there together the afternoon the old man died but she began very strongly to suspect it.

Thoroughly alarmed, she got to wondering what had happened to the Usher cattle. She couldn't turn up one steer marked with Usher's iron and this seemed to her to be uncommonly peculiar. Nesters and mavericks — even, perhaps, a few Indians — might well have accounted for much of this stock, but certainly not for all of it.

She finally went to Frailey. Despite her careful approach to the subject the old doc glanced at her sharply. After a deal of harrumphing he'd made out to allow they'd likely all died off the year of the big blow.

From her father Naome had found out which that was but couldn't bring herself to go further. She ached to get this thing talked out with him but a belated awareness of something glimpsed in his look that time she had taxed him with permitting Churk Crafkin too free a hand sealed her lips. She was suddenly afraid. Afraid, with a terrible dread, of the future.

This was why, at last, she'd gone to Beckwith's office, driven by the reported return of Jake's son to discovering some part of the truth. And there she had found the cancelled checks which had rid the range of Usher's brand.

Fright moved cheek by jowl with her now. She did not dare destroy them — did not dare tell her father. She was afraid, after that clash with Crafkin, to stay at the ranch any longer. She was trapped in a nightmare, scared even to stay at the Buffalo Bull. She was like a man with a bear by the tail, envisioning the awful price of her knowledge. The masks had slipped; there'd be no backing out now. The pattern had almost reached full circle.

Meeting the marshal, Ives Hanna, at breakfast she'd been mightily tempted to put the checks in his care, sealed of course, till she could find a way out of this. If she might only have been sure whose man he was . . . But on the verge of decision she'd seen the ungainly shape of Tularosa entering the store and had fled in blind panic.

Back in her room, badly shaken, she'd gone over what she knew and those things she suspected while mending the leather Churk Crafkin had torn. There'd be no quarter in this, no chance for retrenchment. The stakes were too high. The first false step would fetch death, swift and final.

She must someway get hold of Luke Usher. Even this might not help but it was the only course she could see at the moment. She must talk with him quickly. And it would have to be private.

She went to the window, keeping far enough back to insure her concealment, eyes anxiously searching what she could see of the street. After awhile she saw Tularosa, aboard his horse, ride toward Isham's.

The stage would be coming into town very shortly; she knew her dad might be on it. She left her room, hurrying down Smith's stairs and out into the hot bright smash of the sun. She slipped around to the back, went down a bottle-strewn alley and into the general store by the rear. There was only one clerk in view and he was busy with a customer.

She fingered some yard goods, percale, taffeta, calico. "I'll take some of these, George," she said, "when you're not busy — about eight yards of each. Please wrap them separate."

She picked her way through a clutter of sacked potatoes, barreled flour, crated eggs and stacked tarps, the topmost of which had been recently unfolded and then thrown carelessly back on the pile. Rounding a display of racked rifles she came to where, through a web streaked window, she could see a portion of the street.

She did not locate Tularosa but was satisfied he hadn't departed. He hadn't come to Bella Loma after any load of groceries. She didn't believe he was here to keep an eye out for her father. He'd come after those checks and the knowledge made her desperate.

Two ranch wives with baskets came into the store, their heads sheathed in bonnets, while the clerk was wrapping her cloth up. "You want these charged to the ranch?" he called, and Naome nodded. Then she saw Doc's buggy wheel in to the hitch rack and her heart gave a leap when she beheld Luke Usher reining in behind him.

It was like a great load had been lifted from her shoulders; just the sight of him made her almost light headed. There was a strength in this man that you could feel and rely on.

After that scene with her father she was far from sure Usher's strength was going to help her, but she had to make the try. There was no one else she could turn to. It was more imperative than ever that she talk with him now. He must be made to see the truth and there was no time to lose.

She'd given the bundles to her father, said she'd try to be home tomorrow unless Baisy really needed her, and gone hurrying back to her room at Smith's. She'd take those checks to Usher's ranch. No matter what Luke thought now, once she'd told him her story she should have raised enough doubts to make him want to know more before he unleashed the fury that had been in his eyes when he had looked at her father.

Clad again as he'd first seen her in buckskin and squaw boots, black braids confined in gleaming circlet of wampum, she hurried back to the street and was just about to leave the protection of the buildings when she saw Tularosa. He made a deeper and motionless kind of crouched shadow in the smoky shade flung down by the mesquite whose branches overhung the pingpanging clamor being beaten from Rubelcaba's anvil.

By the slant of his hat she knew the gun fighter's glance was pinned on Isham's in an unswerving stare. He was obviously waiting for her to go fetch her mare.

She drew hesitantly back, but she hadn't much choice. She had to leave town without that leather shipper seeing her and she couldn't afford to risk any further delay.

Predicating all subsequent actions on the presumption Luke Usher had already gone home — which he hadn't — she moved casually forward and, with her heart banging wildly, unloosed the nearest mount from the handiest tie rail. She hauled it into the alley and swung into the saddle. Carefully guiding it through the debris behind buildings, believing she'd eluded Tularosa's vigilance, she sent it into the brush on a shortcut for Usher's.

Marratt never was afterwards able to recall what notion he was worrying when he came into sight of the old Usher ranch house. His mind had been filled with thoughts aroused by Clint Gainor. But the moment he saw the pair of hard-breathing horses standing spraddle-legged before the front porch all the hardness ground into him by experience was apparent. His eyes turned bleak, all the bones of his face standing out like castings.

Those broncs had been pushed and, though grass stood hock deep all over the yard, neither one of the pair had dropped its head to start browsing. If this visit were hostile it didn't look like they'd have left those horses in plain sight. But the men weren't in view and, at this stage of the game, one wrong move could put him out of it for keeps. If these were hirelings of Ryerson . . .

Leaving his animals in the brush at the side of the road, Marratt drew old Jake's pistol and cut around to the barn, moving silently and swiftly. He came in from the rear and moved through it warily without discovering anyone.

Thirty yards of grass-covered open lay between the barn and Jake's back door and he was crouched outside it within twenty seconds, glad he'd forgotten to shut it when he went off with Frailey.

Easing off his boots he stepped into the kitchen. They were in the front room, two open doors beyond and, while he couldn't yet see them because of the angles, he caught the sound of ragged breathing.

"Give 'em here!" growled a voice; and there was a quick rush of bootsteps punctuated by a gasp and the sound of something ripping. He caught the slap of hands against flesh and panting — a sudden curse. Spur rowels rattled above another rush of feet.

Marratt was at the hall door half crouched to go through it when a black-haired girl with the dress half torn off her caromed into his arms, knocking the legs out from under him. He went down hard. His gun flew skittering across the floor. He felt warm flesh against his cheek and shoved her off him, rolling to hands and knees just as the man in pursuit of her, unable to stop, crashed into him.

It fortunately wasn't his bad side which sent the fellow sprawling, but it was plenty bad enough. It knocked him halfway around and left him gagging for air. "Look out —" the girl cried, and the desperation in her voice cut through Marratt's stupor.

He pulled the chin off his chest and saw the fellow unscrambling himself from a wrecked chair. They reeled to their feet at about the same time and the man brought around what was left of the chair in a whistling arc that only missed braining Marratt by inches.

He came alive fast then, sensing the murderous urge that was pushing this fellow, and swaying forward in the whooshing wake of those rungs struck hard as he could at the man's right shoulderblade.

The chair spilled out of Tularosa's grasp. He staggered, striving frantically to keep his balance. Before he could get his feet planted under him Marratt slugged him again, at the point of the left shoulder.

Tularosa slammed into the wall. Something on its far side hit the floor with a crash. But Marratt was too anxious to get his hands on the man. With the wall for leverage Tularosa's brought-up boot took Marratt in the chest and flung him half across the room.

Those shoulder blows had slowed the man up but he came within an ace of getting his gun out of leather before Marratt got back to him. Marratt got hold of that wrist just in time. Even so the gun came out; all Marratt could manage was to deflect the man's aim. That first slug, grazing Marratt's shoulder, brought down the stovepipe in a cloud of soot. The second plowed into the ceiling, but Marratt knew his luck wasn't going to last forever.

He couldn't break the man's hold, couldn't wrest the weapon away from him — the bony gun fighter seemed to have the strength of a tiger and his pistoning left kept battering Marratt's head with a punishment that was reducing Marratt's vision to red fog. There was a ringing in his ears. There were butterflies in his stomach. He finally got his left fist wrapped around that six-inch barrel and, forcing Tularosa's gun arm above his head, attempted to drive the man wallward.

Only then did he commence fully to realize the real nature of what he was up against. It wasn't just that his fellow appeared to have anchored himself to the floor like a leech or that he seemed endowed with three times the strength any man so built could normally count on. A foul stench came out of him, sour with the acrid reek of marihuana — it rose from his sweat like the fumes off a bog; and Marratt began desperately to wonder what chance he stood of coming out of this alive.

His skin started to crawl. He wasn't able during those first harried moments, with all his weight thrown into the struggle, to rock the man from his tracks by one inch. Those crazed white-ringed eyes glaring into his own were filled with the fury of a man gone berserk.

For the first time in his life Marratt experienced the bitter knowledge of fright in all its aspects. His belly trembled, the hinges of his knees seemed on the verge of collapsing; he thought for a moment he was going to throw up.

His grip, rimed with sweat, was beginning to slip and the clubfooted gunman, suddenly abandoning those bludgeoning blows at

139

Marratt's head, directed all his monstrous energy into a series of maneuvers designed to break Marratt's hold on that gun-weighted wrist. He writhed and twisted like a sackful of snakes but, with his arm above his head, he couldn't get enough leverage. He gave backward a step and was carried back another by the thrust of Marratt's weight. He lost his balance and went over, taking Marratt with him, throwing a knee up as he fell.

Marratt thought that knee had gone through his guts, that he was impaled upon the thing with his backbone folded down across it like a dish cloth. Waves of nausea racked him and he retched, never knowing the fellow's wrist had twisted free of fingers that were no longer part of him.

He wanted only to die. Merciful and quick like. There was a brimstone taste to his rag-dry mouth and all the fires of hell were hurling flames across his loins. Yet when he saw the glint of that gun barrel coming he had sense enough left to try and roll away from it.

The blow missed his head but almost took an arm off. He could feel the cold shock all the way to his toenails. Through a haze like spun glass he could see the blue green of the sunlit tamarisks and the curl-patched trunk of the long-leafed eucalyptus beyond the rear door's bright oblong, and down by its thresh-old the shine of Jake's pistol.

He let go of his belly and began to crawl to-ward it.

Something charged across his vision and plowed into something behind him. He heard the gun fighter curse, the scuff of struggling bodies. He didn't stop to look. He locked his eyes straight ahead and kept crawling.

It wasnt till he heard the ragged jump of Naome's breath hit high C in a scream that Marratt jerked his head around. There was blood on Tularosa's gun barrel. Blood's crim-son was lacing through the blue welt beneath the girl's breasts; and it was this which pulled Marratt onto his feet through the reedy crackle of the gunhawk's laughter and slammed him, snarling, at that grotesque shape.

He saw the crazy eyes turn, saw the gun-muzzle lift, saw the flame gouting out of that blood-spattered barrel. He didn't feel the slug's impact. The only thing he had room for was the satisfaction of seeing that pock-marked face rocking backward, eyes enor-mous, from the force with which he'd hit it.

The bony arms flapped outward as the man tried to catch his balance. Sight of the gun still clenched in one fist brought all Marratt's rage boiling up from his bowels. His right caught the barrel, his left grabbed the arm, and he slammed the man's wrist hard against the door's casing. Even through that wild screech he could hear the bones snap. He spun the man around and broke his other wrist also. "Go show those to Bella Loma!"

Then he flung him through the door.

Chapter 12

Naome was watching him when Marratt passed out. He'd retrieved the pistol lost at the outset and, crossing to the door letting into the hall, had been stooping to pick up the one the man had struck her with when the hinges of his knees let go and dropped him, limp, across the boards of the floor.

She did not cry out. She did none of the things a lady would have done, though the memory of Tularosa firing at him point-blank was the most vivid recollection in her mind at that moment. She stepped around Marratt and picked up Tularosa's gun, glad to find when she broke it open its chambered cylinder still held two unfired cartridges.

She went onto the back stoop with the heavy pistol in her hand and looked around for Tularosa without seeing him. Her narrowed glance raked the tamarisks and went ahead of her into the barn without finding any sign of movement. She went on around the house and still could not find him. The borrowed horses were browsing, proof he hadn't gone near them.

Returning, she saw Marratt's boots on the stoop and took them inside. She rolled him carefully over. Tularosa had missed. There was torn cloth edged with blood high up on his left shoulder but examination revealed this to be little more than the track of a powder blast. His collapse had been the result of exhaustion.

She found needle and thread and repaired her appearance as best she was able. She fetched some rags from a cupboard and the half-full bottle of turpentine she'd found while hunting the needle and thread. Unbuttoning Marratt's torn shirt she did what she could for the powder burn and, soaking two of the rags with turpentine, bound them over his chest and stomach just tightly enough to keep them in place.

She righted his overturned table, put the groceries away that were still fit to put away and swept up the rest, including twelve broken eggs it made her sick just to think of. Then she sat down with Tularosa's gun in her lap and waited for the man on the floor to come round.

So this was Luke Usher.

With the chance now to really study his features she tried to find in their lines some indication of the character local repute had ascribed to him. It wasn't the kind of face she would expect to have found on the man who had done what he had fifteen years ago; nor could she make his performance in the Red Horse Bar gee at all with the one she'd just witnessed.

It was all so confusing, so mixed up in her mind. Especially the way her rebellious emotions continually disregarded what her thinking considered irrefutable logic. This man had threatened her father — she had heard him herself this very morning in town. How *could* she — how could any decent girl — feel so drawn toward such a man after remembering the way he had looked on that store porch?

He groaned and she got up and went over to him. "You're all right," she said, "just take it easy." She helped him onto his feet.

"Close that back door," he grumbled. "Did you take care of my horses?"

She looked surprised. "I didn't see any horses but those two in the yard."

He told her where he'd left them and while she was gone he got into his boots. When she came back he was in the front room stretched out on the couch underneath Jake's picture. The resemblance was startling. "Is that old Jake?" she asked.

Marratt nodded.

"I shouldn't think, after what I said to your father —"

"We'll talk of that later."

She went back to the kitchen, put the stovepipe together, swept the place out again and went outside and washed up. She built up a fire and while she worked she went over in her mind what she would say to him. She was not shocked by what he had done to Tularosa; all her thoughts were concerned with what he might do to her father if she failed to convince him. She looked in on him once while the meal was cooking and found him asleep.

When she had everything on the table she called him. He came in from the back, having detoured to wash and slick back his hair with his fingers, cowpuncher fashion. He surprised her by returning thanks and still further astonished her by passing everything her way before helping himself.

When they were finished Marratt pushed back his plate. Their eyes met and locked and something stronger than themselves pulled them onto their feet and his hands gripped her shoulders. They stared at one another, Naome's eyes frightened, questioning; Marratt's hungrily demanding. Their lips met and clung and then she pushed him away and

Marratt said, inexplicably bitter: "You came out here because of what I said to your father?"

"Of course. You're wrong about Dad — terribly wrong."

"Did you fetch that gun fighter along to persuade me?"

"I didn't fetch him. I came to give you those checks I took from Beckwith's office. Tularosa came out hoping to get them away from me."

"And succeeded, of course, so that —"

"No. I still have them."

Marratt looked at her awhile, his bearded cheeks inscrutable.

"I find that somewhat hard to follow. The cattle those checks paid for were stolen by Wineglass. Ryerson owns Wineglass; Jake Usher owned those cattle. You took the checks to protect your father, yet you claim to've come out here to give them to me. It doesn't make sense."

"I think it will if you'll listen —"

"You could have given them to me yesterday."

"I didn't know you yesterday."

"You knew who I was this morning."

"But I hadn't decided then what to do with them. It was what you said to Dad that —"

"Does your father know you've got them?"

"He doesn't even dream they exist."

"Yet he sends this gunhawk —"

"If anyone sent Tularosa it was Crafkin —"

"Crafkin. Tularosa." Marratt's smile was starved and wintry. "What difference does it make? They both draw their pay and get their orders from Ryerson."

She considered him a moment. "I'm going to show you where you're wrong," she said. "While they both get their pay out of Wineglass, neither of them takes any orders from Dad. For a proper slant on what has happened around here you must understand, in the first place, that my father has spent half his life on a dream. On a quest for the pot at the foot of the rainbow."

"A romantic notion," Marratt said. He fished out the makings.

Naome's chin came up. "Call it foolish if you want to. The essential fact is still true. In the last seventeen years he's been around Bella Loma very little. He's never cared for ranching; always he's been sure he's going to uncover some lost bonanza." She brushed a strand of black hair back away from her cheek. "You must have known people like that."

Marratt didn't say whether he had or he hadn't. He lighted his cigarette, lifting and lowering his shoulders, his attention seeming more absorbed with the girl herself than with the thoughts she was attempting to put into words.

"You've got to listen to me, Luke," she said half-angrily. "That's the way my father *is* — it's part of the explanation of how things around us here came to be as we find them. He has never cared a snap of his fingers for ranching. Because he loved her my father married an Indian woman who was able to share his nomadic life happily. To allow him more time to do as he wanted he hired Churk Crafkin to manage the ranch. He literally turned it over to him lock, stock and barrel."

Marratt still didn't speak but she could see that he was thinking.

"I don't want to labor the point, but you have to believe that to understand what's been happening. He has never, to my knowledge, demanded any accounting or asked one question of Crafkin. The man's like a king; he does just as he pleases — in the name of Clem Ryerson. And my father reaps the blame!"

She went on then to tell him of the things she'd discovered, concluding with the story of her visit to Beckwith's office, her finding of the checks, her waylayal by Crafkin and subsequent flight to town. She told how, badly frightened, she had taken the room at Smith's and of, this morning, seeing

Tularosa. "Beckwith must have looked for those checks and sent word right away to Crafkin."

"But when he stopped you in that gulch I don't see how he could have known —"

"He didn't, of course; he wasn't after the checks then. He was trying," she said, flushing, "to put me in the right frame of mind to accept him for a husband — can't you see what he's been up to? what his goal's been all along? He's after Wineglass! If he can't get it by forcing me into a marriage — I know it sounds incredible but the man's an incredible person. He's utterly ruthless, and I think he suspects —"

"But the only real evidence you've got is those checks," Marratt said. "It just doesn't make sense. If he's the kind of a two-legged polecat you're painting he'd have himself so protected on that deal with Beckwith that the only one those checks could incriminate would be your father. They'd be made out to Wineglass."

"They are," Naome said.

"So you're presuming a kickback that can't be proved. If it ever came to court it'd be his word against Ryerson's —"

"Now you've arrived at my own conviction, the thought which sent me after them. Since they'd almost certainly be made out to Wineglass and would therefore convict my father, whom everyone around here considers an un-principled range hog, I knew, when I heard you'd come back, I'd have to destroy them. What I had overlooked — what you and Churk Crafkin have, too, for that matter — is the character of the man who was buying those cattle." She came back and dropped into her chair.

"What about it?"

"Ask yourself — you talked to him."

Marratt nodded. The lids of his eyes squeezed down a little.

"I see what you mean. The man's a born double-crosser whose every instinct would be to protect himself. So he marked them when they came back from the bank."

Naome pulled off one of her boots and passed them over.

But after studying them awhile Marratt shook his head. "This might tend to show Stanley Beckwith's good faith. It won't help your father."

"With those notations?" Naome said un-easily, "Why won't it?"

"Because even though this shows they were Usher cattle Beckwith bought from your range boss, Crafkin will say he was only fol-lowing instructions and delivered them to Beckwith on Ryerson's orders. Things being

151

as they are, no matter what your father says folks are going to take Crafkin's word —"

"The *bank* won't take it," Naome broke in heatedly, "and when the bank's records are fetched into court no one else in his right mind is going to take it either. Churk Crafkin endorsed every one of those checks and not a penny of that money ever went into the ranch accounts!"

"If you can prove that it may get your father off, but —"

"You still think he was back of it?" Naome's glance locked with Marratt's incredulously. "After all I've told you and —"

"I'll give him the benefit of the doubt on the cow deal, but you've said yourself he was on this ranch the day old Jake —"

"So was Crafkin! Can't you see how it all hangs together?"

"I can see how you'd like it to," Marratt conceded. "I'm not blaming you. If I were you I'd feel the same. You've built up a good case but that's all it is — theory. Just a lot of slick guesswork —"

"And what do you call what you've built up against my father? Did you actually see him *shoot* Jake Usher?"

Marratt stared at her a moment. "No. I didn't see him shoot Jake —"

"But you told everyone he did it! If I'd maligned anybody the way you have him I'd certainly feel responsible for finding out the truth! Or are you," she said bitterly, "afraid to find out — afraid to go up against a man who's made a career of killing?"

Marratt's eyes turned bleak. But before he could answer they heard the sound of a buggy coming into the yard. Naome jumped up. She leaned across the table and snatched up the checks. She said suddenly, fiercely: "If you go on with your intentions with regard to my father I'll see you in hell if it's the last thing I do!"

Chapter 13

Hoof sound and buggy wheels stopped outside the door. Brown eyes still showing the
seething violence of her emotions, Naome
jerked it open. Frailey's face appeared, surprised, hung indecisively there a moment
and looked about to be withdrawn when
Marratt growled, "We ain't got nothing
that's catching."

The old medico looked uncomfortable. "I
could just as well come back later, Luke . . ."

"No need to do that. Miss Ryerson's about
to leave anyway. Would you care for a cup of
java?"

Naome thrust the checks at the doctor. "I
wonder if you'd mind keeping these for me?"

As Frailey reached to take them Marratt
said, stubbing out his smoke, "Never heard
you express your convictions on the subjects
of life and death, Doc, but if you ain't in no
hurry to meet your Maker I'd suggest you
stick to rolling pills."

The girl's face turned, threw an irritated glance at him.

Marratt said, ignoring its message, "You should know what you're getting into. Those pretty green papers are coffin bait, Doc. They're the checks paid by Beckwith for stolen Usher cattle."

Frailey's wrinkled cheeks sagged with a variety of emotions, the most discernible of which appeared to be shock. He seemed to be having a little trouble with his breathing if one could judge by the way he tugged at his collar.

Marratt said to Naome, "Don't ask him to go into a thing like that blind. Tell him what you told me and let him do his own thinking."

As she told him the story the doctor's countenance, schooled by many a crisis, revealed nothing of his thoughts but grew steadily more grave, particularly when she came to Marratt's fight with Tularosa.

When she was done he did not speak at once but appeared to be turning it over. He said at last, "I've long suspected that fellow Crafkin had a pretty free hand in the things that have made your father unpopular —"

"Then you believe I'm right?" Naome asked breathlessly. "You think, as I do, it was Crafkin who really killed Luke's father?"

Frailey hesitated. "I believe it was Crafkin who pushed Wineglass expansion, who built the spread up to its present size and power, and I believe he did this with the intention of eventually taking it over. But —"

"If you concede that much you've got to admit he killed Luke's father — it's all of a pattern. And he was here that day. He had the opportunity."

The doctor said, frowning, "We have only your conviction on that point, Naome. I happen to know your father made several offers for this property —"

"Dad? Or Wineglass?"

Frailey looked uncomfortable. "The most of them may have come through Crafkin, but your father made at least one of them because I was here myself and heard him. He offered Jake ten thousand dollars for the place without the stock."

"There was nothing wrong with that price or with him offering it," Naome countered.

"It suggests he was determined to have it —"

"Not necessarily. It borders our ranch on this side and if Crafkin persuaded Dad we might have trouble over the boundaries . . . You've got to realize that Dad took Crafkin's word unreservedly on anything having to do with the running of Wineglass. If Crafkin said we had to have this place Dad probably thought it would avoid ill feeling if he offered

Jake more than the ranch was worth. Jake Usher's stubbornness was proverbial from what I've been told. They say he was very hot-headed and very —"

"Yes, he was proud and hot-headed, and he was stubborn," Frailey said, "and if your father and Crafkin did come over here that day, there might very well have been trouble."

His frowning eyes touched Marratt's face. "You made some pretty wild statements that day yourself, Luke. Has your memory been able to dig up the sight of Ryerson shooting —"

"No," Marratt said.

"Did you see Ryerson or Crafkin here that day?"

"I have no recollection of it."

"Were you here when your father was shot?"

"I —" Marratt said instead, "It seems to me to be highly suggestive that, if Ryerson and Crafkin were here when Jake was killed, neither one of them has ever seen fit to admit it."

"It seems suggestive to *me*," Naome came back sharply, "that you've never said why you accused Dad — never offered the least evidence in support of your charge!"

Frailey's eyes, too, looked the question.

Marratt's cheeks remained inscrutable.

Frailey said to Naome, "I'd like to make it plain —"

Marratt lifted a hand. "Somebody coming."

Naome's face twisted doorward. The doctor looked that way, too. The sound of a walking horse rounded the house and stopped in the back yard and a man's voice called: "Anybody home?"

Marratt stepped around Frailey and went out on the stoop. The man on the horse said, "Your name Usher?"

"What's on your mind?"

"Heard you might be figurin' to open up again so I reckoned I'd drop by an' test the chances of a job." He sat his horse like a man who'd been born to the saddle but his long-fingered hands showed little acquaintance with a rope and were too well kept to belong to a range hand. He wore benchmade boots and blue serge pants that were powdered with dust and showed the glint of long usage. The coat to the pants was on his back, hanging open to reveal a shirt designed for a stiff collar which he had apparently discarded. He had straw-colored hair and a straw colored mustache; but it was the bone-handled gun that Marratt looked at the longest. That, and the half-amused slanch of green stare.

"Gainor send you?"

"Don't know any Gainor. Do I have to get the okey from him to get a job here?"

"Mostly," Marratt said, "you've got to be able to work a gun." He was conscious of the girl stepping out of the door behind him and of the bold and lecherous way those arrogant eyes assessed her figure. "On the barn door behind you there's a piece of strap iron that gets by for a hasp —"

The report of the pistol jumped through his words. Sixty feet away the hasp banged round on its swivel and the richocheting slug screamed to silence over the tamarisks. Smooth and swift as had been its drawing the fellow's gun was snugged in leather.

"Try it again," Marratt said and, ignoring the coat-wearer's look, watched carefully. He saw no more than before, a mere blur of motion culminating in thunder. The hasp remained static but the hole the slug drilled wasn't two inches from it.

He watched the empties punched out and replaced with live cartridges. "You been long around here?"

The green eyes grinned. "Not long enough to get in no trouble."

Marratt's sinews pulled tight as a shaggy-haired pup came around the barn's side and, answering the man's whistle, trotted over and sat down, ears pricked and tongue lolling.

"Is that your dog?" Naome asked.

"Never saw him before."

"He seemed to know your whistle."

"Looks to me like anybody's dog that'll call him."

Marratt whistled. The dog came over and sat down with his tail happily thumping the stoop.

"Just dog," the stranger said in a tone bordering smugness. "Do I get that job or don't I?"

"For as long as it lasts," Marratt said, "you've got it." He scowled at the discoloring knuckles of his hands. "Turn your cayuse in with those others and stash your truck in the old man's bedroom." About to start off he swung back, saying sourly, "What name do you want burnt onto your headboard?"

The green eyes laughed. "Kid Boots will look good as anything, I reckon. But don't get me planted till I been cut down."

Marratt strode past the girl and went into the house. He didn't care what label a drifting slug-slammer gave himself; it was the tail-wagging part of the yard's assemblage he was scowling about. That dog might come to anyone's call but it was still the same pup he'd seen by that tank when he'd come onto Naome swimming in the raw.

At Wineglass Clem Ryerson, in his room

with the door shut, was squatted before a cast-iron safe sifting through a batch of reports and clippings having mainly to do with folks who'd once lived in Texas. He leafed through them again with a nervous care.

Frowning, he thrust them back in their envelope, dropping it into a metal drawer which he carefully closed and locked. Methodically, then, he started through the safe's pigeonholes, finally with a grunt going back to his desk with a yellowing page of newsprint carrying a five-year-old Prescott dateline. Smoothing this out he stared a long while at the pair of cuts accompanying a two-column item headed: U.S. MARSHAL VICTIM OF LOCAL RANCHER.

Rummaging his desk he produced a partly-filled bottle of ancient ink, a screaky-nibbed pen and several sheets of blank paper and, with a bleak expression, wrote in a crabbed left-handed scrawl for upwards of ten minutes. He then folded the sheet of newsprint and put it with his writing in an envelope which, after considerable thought, he addressed to the governor.

Thrusting this envelope into his pocket Ryerson closed the safe, gave the knob a quick flip, and picked up his hat. He hadn't seen a soul since he'd got back to the ranch and, just at the moment, he didn't want to see anyone.

He went out the back way and climbed onto his horse. He stared a moment or two in the direction of Bella Loma, then reversed the long-limbed speedy looking grulla and took off for Casa Grande.

On the kitchen table beside his pushed-back plate Marratt saw a sheaf of banknotes which he picked up with some surprise. But as he stared at the crisp new bills in his hands his thoughts left the dog and his new serge-suited employee. "Hey, Doc!" he called, hurrying into the front room; but Frailey had gone.

He thrust the currency into his pocket. It was the loan they'd gone to town for. The old medico had left him the whole two hundred.

Naome came into the room. She said, "I wouldn't put too much trust in that fellow."

"Did you give Frailey those checks?"

Her look met his defiantly. "I don't think, Luke Usher, you have any right to ask."

Marratt's lips pulled in a bit tighter at their corners but he couldn't leave it there. "At least take my advice and get rid of them. Don't keep them on you. If Crafkin was back of Tularosa he's not going to —"

"Then you *do* believe —"

"Look," Marratt said. "No matter what's the straight of that deal in Usher cattle, those

162

cattle were stolen and Beckwith's checks prove it. You might just as well lug around a live rattler —"

"That wasn't the impression you gave me a little while ago."

"I'm getting a wider look at this now. I believe you're right about Crafkin rigging that cow steal. If you should also be right about him figuring to take the spread over, the smartest thing you could do from here on out is to stay plumb away from there."

Some of the tightness went out of Naome's cheeks. Something changed in her eyes and she said with a shy impulsiveness, "You mean — you want me to stay here?"

"Lord, no! Stay in town where you'll have some protection. You must know *someone* you could stay with."

"Well, there's Clint Gainor's wife . . ."

Marratt stared like he couldn't believe he was hearing it.

"Of course," Naome said, "she's not in town exactly, but —"

"Go to Chandler or Casa Grande. Get put up in a room at some prominent hotel and stay out of sight until this thing's been ironed out."

She considered him carefully. "You mean to go after Crafkin?"

"I can't tell," he said flatly, "what I'm going

to do. But if I've got to be watching out for you all the time —"

"You won't," Naome said with her chin coming up. "My place is with my father and I shall stay right with him until I know where you stand on the matter of Jake Usher."

He was too goaded, too harried by the hell of his thoughts, to give any proper care to his words. "You'll be with him on a slab at some undertakin' parlor if you don't stop getting in Churk Crafkin's hair!" He glared at her angrily. "Can't you get it through your head that going out there now you'll be playing right into that bastard's hands?"

"I can see that the things I've told you about him haven't made the least difference in your attitude toward Dad!"

Something warned him to go easy but the bit was in his teeth now and his tongue was in top gear. With a kind of shocked horror he heard his fool mouth telling her, "What's between your father and me ain't got nothing to do with Jake Usher or Crafkin or anything else that's happened around here. Go tell him that if you want to — and you can tell him from me that the next time we meet he better come a-smokin'!"

Chapter 14

Long after the girl had gone Marratt sat in the darkening front of Jake's house and bitterly thought how right Doc had been when the old man had prophesied there would be no tomorrow in this country for him.

The cards had been stacked from the very beginning, from the moment he'd walked in on Charlie and found her — from the moment he'd lined his sights on that marshal. He'd been licked right then and he'd known it. But what choice had he had? Could any man who called himself one have done different?

He'd been over this before and he still had to shake his head.

Perhaps he needn't have got into this mess at Bella Loma. But that had looked like the hand of Providence then, a good chance to hide out from the law till he could pick up the trail of Clagg's partner. And if he hadn't stepped into the boots of Luke Usher he might have gone straight away, never guessing his quarry was the big mogul round here.

In some ways, he thought, it was too bad he hadn't.

But that was weakness, the natural wish to see shifted to other shoulders the awful responsibility which the luck of discovery had shoved on his own. For the law would never worry Hugh Clagg — he'd seen that much. It would have been Marratt's word, and unsupported at that, against the say of a federal marshal. The girl was dying when he found her, dying of her own hand because . . . You couldn't take a thing like that into court. No one could. No one decent.

And so he'd hunted Clagg down and killed him, shot him just the way he would have shot a mad dog.

Could he do less to Naome's father?

There was no use thinking he might have gotten Charlie's words wrong. She had described them both while she'd lain sobbing in his arms; the three-fingered man, she'd said, had been Clagg's partner.

When you were dealing with facts you had to look them in the face. If anything Clem Ryerson, with a daughter like Naome, had less excuse than Clagg.

Maybe Ryerson hadn't touched her. If he'd been framed in the Bella Loma deal — and it looked as though he had been — might he not also have been framed in this? But Charlie had described him; and there was a sameness to the pattern. If you believed the one could you deny the other?

Ryerson had gone with his range boss to visit old Jake who had subsequently died with a slug through his skull. But had Ryerson come forward? No, he'd kept his mouth shut. Just as he had kept his mouth shut at Prescott.

Across the screen of Marratt's mind flashed the remembered look of Ryerson's daughter as they'd got up from the table and he had gripped her shoulders. There'd been a kind of shining compulsion about her and he realized now that she had wanted him to kiss her, welcoming his passion and wanting him to know how much she had to offer. The wild shock of that embrace, the solid feel of her against him . . .

There was a time for thinking and a time for action, and the time when thought could help was gone beyond recall.

He heard Kid Boots come into the house and carry his belongings into Jake's bedroom and go back to the porch; and he heard the dry screak of his weight in Jake's rocker.

Marratt sighed in the darkness and reluctantly got up. He rolled big shoulders together, clamped jaws on his resolve and, putting behind him the things he could not change, dragged his big-roweled spurs to the porch's screen door. "Is there a horse still browsing the grass out yonder?"

"If there is he's bein' damn quiet about it." Kid Boots said after a moment, "That girl, when she left, took an extra bronc with her. You want me to go after it?"

"No," Marratt said, "I want you to stay right where you're at."

"That's the kind of a job I can stand a whole lot of. Rockin' my time away an' bein' paid for it. You must be well heeled."

"I'm riding into Bella Loma. Any visitors you may get while I'm gone will be trespassers to be dealt with according to the degree of their hostility. And don't be surprised unless you're hankering to get planted."

Going back through the house Marratt crossed to the corrals and, getting down his rope, put a loop on the apron-faced roan he'd got from Isham. After cinching on his rig and climbing into the saddle, he took a moment to examine the loads in Jake's pistol. Then he walked the horse around to the front.

Kid Boots' guarded hail came out of the porch shadows. "Expectin' anyone special?"

"Fellow named Gainor might decide to pay us a call. I think he kind of imagines he's got an interest in this outfit."

"He just imagines it, eh?"

"I'm keeping this place unencumbered."

"What about Wineglass?"

Marratt said, very soft, "What about it?"

"From the talk I've picked up they been usin' this spread. That all right with you?"

"When it isn't," Marratt said, "I'll make sure you're informed."

The lights of Bella Loma threw a lonesome shine across the dust of its single street when Marratt rode in and pulled up near the general store. Frailey's second-floor office and dispensary were reached by an uncovered outside staircase. Marratt observed a number of still-saddled horses dozing hipshot before the town's four saloons and, above the dark store, a reading lamp's golden circle made a halo of brightness behind a drawn shade.

He took the stairs quietly, having no way of knowing what he might be about to run into. But the doctor was alone. He came to the door with a book in his hand, seemed a bit surprised but invited him in.

When the door was closed he said, "Nothing wrong, is there?"

"Nothing a couple lead pills won't cure. I came after those checks."

Frailey, in shirtsleeves, went over and got a cigar from a case in his coat. With a sharp little knife he amputated the end he planned to put in his mouth. "Air in this country plays hell with these things," he growled, carefully licking frayed edges of wrapper. "Naome tell you I had them?"

"I don't want to get rough but if you make me I'll take 'em."

"Reckon at that I'd fare better than I would with Churk Crafkin." Frailey handed them over. "Mind saying what you want with them?"

"I'd like, if I can, to pull some of the heat off Naome. She's let me believe she's on her way back to Wineglass."

Frailey lowered his cigar. "Do you consider that wise?"

"Of course it ain't wise. It's about the dumbest damn thing she could do; but she's stubborn." He looked about to say more, but he didn't.

Frailey said, "And where do the checks —"

"Crafkin, naturally, is wild to get his hands on them."

"You think he knows about Beckwith's notations?"

"He's going to know about them," Marratt said grimly, "and he's going to know I've got them just as quick as some bar fly can fetch him the news. You got any mucilage? You got a sheet of white paper?"

Frailey produced them.

Marratt picked out the check that was for the greatest amount of money and, careful to leave the end free which showed Crafkin's endorsement, stuck the other end of it to one side of the paper, length-wise. "Now, if you've got a marking crayon . . ."

The doctor got one off his desk and Marratt, making his letters big and black, printed beneath it: A WARNING TO SKUNKS.

"That won't scare him off," Frailey said. "Put that up in the Red Horse Bar and you've shown this country he's a crook all right but you've lost any chance of ever getting a conviction. You're selling Crafkin short. He'll tear it up and laugh in your face."

"He'll tear it up," Marratt nodded, "but he won't do no laughing till he's torn up the rest of them. And while he's trying to do that he won't be bothering Naome."

"He'll be bothering *you.* He'll come down on you like the side of a mountain. Every hired gun on his payroll will be after your scalp. You understand that, don't you?"

"You worry too much, Doc," Marratt said, getting up.

"Don't imagine," Frailey said, "I think you're reaching for any halo. Sticking out your own neck isn't diminishing by a particle the mental anguish you're inflicting on that girl. What have you got against her father? Why are you so obsessed —"

"Aren't you forgetting old Jake?"

"You don't care two hoots whether he killed Jake or not. You haven't made the slightest effort —"

"Maybe you know what you're talking about —"

"You better believe that," Frailey said gruffly. "You're no more Luke Usher than I am."

Marratt went still with his throat dry as cotton; and then, bleakly, he grinned. He lowered a hip to the desk and met Frailey's eyes straightly. "That's right. I'm Grete Marratt."

Frailey's eyes narrowed slightly. "The Prescott marshal-killer?"

"Right again."

"Seems to me I did hear something about you breaking out of Yuma. You came through, I presume, hoping to strike some section of border where the authorities wouldn't expect your appearance. You looked about half starved the night I found you; so I imagine you must have stopped for grub and someone, obviously thinking you were Luke, tried to kill you. After I came along and made the same mistake —"

"I figured," Marratt nodded, "I might just as well *be* Luke. I needed a place to hole up

172

and being Luke Usher seemed a lot less dangerous than —"

"I can understand that," Frailey said. "The thing I don't get is your attitude toward Ryerson."

Marratt's look turned bleak. But the doctor, watching with eyes that had diagnosed many ailments, sensed the terrible pressure behind those locked jaws. Wisely he waited and Marratt suddenly rasped harshly, "Did you follow the trial? Did you wonder why I'd killed Clagg — why I made no defense?"

"I thought perhaps there was a woman —"

"It was a girl. Just a kid — a fourteen-year-old orphan girl whose folks had been neighbors of mine till some half-drunk Pimas came onto them one night and rubbed them out, scalping both of them. The girl was away, visiting an aunt at the time; and when she got back I helped her bury them. She was a pretty little trick, big for her age and plucky — they don't come more plucky than that girl was. I had tried to get her to go live with her aunt but she said no, she would be all right there. She went ahead by herself and put in a planting, forty acres of alfalfa which I'd agreed to buy from her; had it just about ready for cutting when this Clagg come along."

Marratt stopped for a moment. Frailey, watching with gray cheeks, saw the way the big bones shone through the skin of his fists. He didn't speak and Marratt said, "After Clagg left she'd tried to shoot herself. She hadn't done a good job but even a poor one will serve if enough blood is spilled."

He swallowed hard a couple of times. "She was on her last gasp when I found her. There'd been two of them, this badge-packer and an older skunk which she said was his partner. I got their descriptions. After she'd slipped away and I had fixed her up as good as I could, I fetched a couple of my men and a sodbuster she'd known and we buried her.

"The boys thought it was an accident and I never said no different. I knew this marshal was in the country. I let a couple of weeks slide by so there wouldn't be no talk, then I went after him."

Frailey said at last, and his voice sounded like he might have got smoke up his windpipe, "Man, you didn't have to go to Yuma for that. They'd have —"

"Would you have dragged her shame through all of those papers? through all those weeks of ranting and jawing?"

Marratt pulled his hip off the desk and took a turn about the room. "All the time I was in prison I kept thinking about that other guy, that older devil that had got clean away. And I watched my chance. I knew from the girl's description of his rig that he had come from the south, from the desert country. I didn't know until this morning, when you introduced him to me —"

"But a *description*," Frailey growled. "That's a hell of a thing to stake a man's life on!"

"I've been over it a hundred times in my mind since I ran into him on that store porch this morning. The description fits. She said he was older than the one with the badge. She said 'a three-fingered man with an uptilted nose and the track of a scar across his left temple'."

"Just the same, you're not God. You don't know that he —"

"Could she have described him, do you think, if he hadn't been there? She called him the marshal's partner."

Frailey shook his head. "I've known Clem Ryerson for thirty years and I tell you, frankly, I can't believe it. Consider Naome. She was left without a mother before she was hardly out of swaddling clothes; her whole outlook is the result of Ryerson's companionship and guidance. If the man had that kind of quirk in his character —"

"Does one person ever truly understand completely the hidden depths of another's nature? How do you explain Usher's killing?"

Frailey chewed on his cigar. "I have never

believed Ryerson killed Jake Usher; nor do I now. I'll admit he might conceivably have done so. Given the right set of conditions almost any man will kill. Circumstances or Crafkin — perhaps even Jake himself, may have backed Ryerson into a corner. Jake was my friend but he was proud and sometimes arrogant; his temper was notorious. If Ryerson happened to be around that day —"

"He was there. The girl admits it."

"Then, as I say, he *might* have shot Jake. But there's no parallel, Marratt, between a man in a corner shooting himself out of it and the picture you've painted of him aiding and abetting the molestation of a child."

"I think there is," Marratt said. "In the two situations we have an identical set of facts. In the first we have Ryerson going with Crafkin to Usher's house, and Usher's subsequent death. In the second we have Ryerson going with Clagg to the house of a girl who is subsequently shamed into taking her own life. In each situation we have Ryerson's stated presence and Ryerson's complete unprincipled silence. I would call that quite a parallel."

Frailey was shaken. His face showed it. But he could be stubborn too, and he growled, "I still say you're not God, Marratt. You've no right to take over His province. Even if you've hit on the truth of this matter there is still

Ryerson's daughter — have you thought about her?"

"Why do you think," Marratt snarled, "I'm going to put up this paper? I'll take care of Crafkin —"

"Do you imagine 'taking care' of Crafkin will be adequate compensation for what you plan to do to her father? That girl's in love with you, Marratt —"

He broke off, eyes staring, as feet drummed sound from the outside stairs. A voice cried: *"Luke!"* and they stood as though frozen while the door burst open to disclose Naome, the black mop of her hair tumbled about by the wind, the whole look of her telling how near she'd come to hysteria.

"They've got him!"

Chapter 15

"You mean your *father?*"

Marratt stared at the girl with disbelieving eyes. It seemed incredible that Crafkin, before getting hold of those checks, would risk the whole structure of all he had schemed for by laying violent hands on the man who had made it all possible. He said as much and Frailey, intent on reassuring her, nodded. "He's probably gone off on another prospecting trip."

"In his good clothes? Without a word?" Her probing stare searched their faces. "I don't believe it. Luke coming home and then those checks right on top of it and Tularosa crippled . . . I tell you Crafkin's frightened! There wasn't a soul at the ranch and Dad's safe's been broken open — there were papers all over the floor!"

"It don't make sense," Marratt grumbled, picking up the surprise he'd got ready for Crafkin and thrusting the three loose checks in his pocket. "But if you'll stay here with Doc I'll go out there —"

"And get Dad away from them?"

Frailey said hurriedly, "He can't answer that until he finds what he's up against. The whole thing may be a ruse . . ."

Naome, still with her face watching Marratt's, said: "Will you?"

She has him over a barrel, Frailey thought; and the torment, the anguished gleam of Marratt's eyes confirmed it.

With a strangled cry he incontinently fled, recklessly plunging down the dark stairs.

But at their bottom he pulled up, his mind taking hold of the doctor's words. It *could* be a ruse; yet even as he conceded this he discovered the flaw in such an assumption. Crafkin, if he had been trying to trap Usher, would have used the girl — not her father.

Irascibly Marratt shoved a hand through his hair, and wondered what the hell had become of his hat. It was one of those irrelevancies which sometimes seem so important in a crisis though you know all the time they have no right usurping thought so direly needed elsewhere.

He struck out toward the lights of the Red Horse Bar, deciding he had probably left it at Doc's.

But if the girl had been right about them

grabbing her father Crafkin would have had no reason to break open that safe. Someone else, of course, might have done it. Someone, like Naome, who had gone out there and found the place deserted.

Gainor?

In the press of other things he had forgotten Clint Gainor with his sly little eyes and his gun-backed demand to be taken into partnership as pay for his silence. His greed might be due for a considerable shock when and if he got around to checking up on Usher's signature.

Shoving through the saloon's batwings he looked the place over with a hard wintry stare which failed to discover the least sign of anything hostile among the assembled half dozen who were bellying the bar.

He could not fail to note the sudden way they quit talking but, ignoring this and them along with it, he approached the scarred oak and beckoned the apron.

The man's spraddled lips showed a parched kind of smiling. "H'are you, Mr. Usher? We heard you was back. Figurin' to put the old place on its feet again?"

"I'd like to borrow a knife," Marratt said — "a good sharp one."

"You want to pare your nails, maybe?"

"A skinning knife, I think, would be nearer what I'm after."

The bartender's eyes turned a little apprehensive. He slanched a look at the wholly-still wooden-faced customers. "Any you boys got a skinnin' knife on you?"

Someone produced one. He shuffled off to get it. The gleam of sweat was on his cheeks and damply beading his flaccid jowls as he came back and reluctantly laid it down before Marratt.

Marratt got out his *warning to skunks* and, with the knife, silently skewered it to one of the posts holding up the tin ceiling. With a final inscrutable glance he walked out.

He got aboard his roan horse and stepped it past the saloon which the town marshal favored without seeing the man. He was wheeling the horse around, about to strike out for Wineglass, when a small dark man came up out of the shadows. "Your name Usher?"

"And if it is?" Marratt said.

"I been asked to tell you your crew'll show up tomorrow forenoon. You better lay in some grub and a couple dozen gross of boxed cartridges —"

"Just a minute," Marratt called. "I'm not expecting any crew."

"You are now," the man grinned.

Marratt dropped folded hands across the pommel of his saddle. "Who put you up to this?"

"I guess you know who's holdin' your paper. Grub he said get, an' a wagonload of cartridges."

"All right," Marratt scowled — "now you high-tail it back to him. You tell him I said his cinch is getting frayed and without he's craving to get a leg tied up he better make a wide loop around my spread in the future."

"I'll tell him," the man nodded, "but you better be expecting them boys tomorrow mornin'."

"If they come out," Marratt promised, "it'll be to stay permanent."

He set out for Wineglass at a ground-eating canter. There was no moon riding herd on the range but a sky full of stars gave him all the light he needed to pick out a trail by. He still could not convince himself Churk Crafkin was responsible for Ryerson's reported absence. If the man was really gone it seemed a heap more likely he'd taken fright from Marratt's remarks and decided to pull a bolt.

This thought caused Marratt to grit his teeth, but he was not too taken up with thinking about Ryerson to overlook the possible consequences of running onto Crafkin. He fully shared Naome's conviction that the Wineglass segundo was the man to be reckoned with. No one with the perseverence of

Crafkin was going to take all this meddling without retaliation; and he was inclined to lay the reputed absence of the crew more to some new move on the part of its ramrod than to any connection it might have with Clagg's partner.

One thing he could bank on. If Tularosa had fetched his broken wrists back to Crafkin, the man wouldn't be in any mood to yell boo at. He'd be out for blood and no mistake about that.

Marratt tried for awhile to think which way the cat would jump. While he could not pin anything down for certain, it seemed increasingly evident that before he was much older he'd be facing Ives Hanna, the Wineglass-owned town marshal.

Time was running out.

Marratt had no way of guessing how many miles he'd put behind him when he became acutely conscious of the smell of risen dust. Casting back he felt sure he'd caught whiffs of it before and, while the fact itself did not unduly perturb him, he was alarmed to discover he could so long have ignored it. Carelessness of that sort could get a man rubbed out.

There was another rider ahead of him someplace. Since the fellow was patently bound in the same direction it was probably someone who'd quit town just ahead of him. Someone packing the news from the Red Horse Bar.

He hauled the roan down to an easier gait. He had no desire to interfere with this traveler. The whole purpose of that *warning to skunks* he'd hung up had been to channel Crafkin's rage away from Naome. That it would center on himself was a foregone conclusion and exactly what he'd aimed for. Taking care of Churk Crafkin was the least he could do, considering the fate he had in mind for Clem Ryerson.

Once again Frailey's words grimly tramped through his thinking and Marratt bitterly cursed.

He had increasingly to buttress his resolve with visions of Charlie and not even the ghastliness of these could wholly purge his thoughts of Naome. She, too, had a claim and honesty forced him to acknowledge that hers might be the greater; but this in no way lessened the ugly fact of Ryerson's guilt.

Every trail Marratt's conjectures so hopefully embarked on angled inevitably back to that. Ryerson had been there else how could the girl have described him? She had called him the badge-packer's partner, and thus was his guilt established. He did not need to have touched her; he'd been there and hadn't stopped Clagg. More damning still was his subsequent silence. Those locked lips were the proof of his complicity.

For twenty minutes after climbing out of timber Marratt's roan had been following the convolutions of a bluff, picking its way between pear and cholla. Now, abruptly rounding its western flank, Marratt thought, a bit startled, to catch the rumor of gunfire. He pulled up and sat listening without hearing anything further.

Naome'd been wrong — he knew that — in assuming because she'd found the ranch deserted her father's foreman had turned wolf. He would turn wolf all right but when he did, Marratt thought, it wouldn't be to run down game as puny as the man he'd used for camouflage all these years.

Just the same, suddenly worried, Marratt sent the roan forward. That rider whose discovered dust had caused him to drop back need not, because he'd thought it was, be a currier from the Red Horse Bar — it could have been Naome! She'd had ample time to leave town ahead of him; he hadn't noticed her horse when he'd gone back to get his own.

He used his spurs on the roan, unaccountably disquieted. They swept around a tangle of chaparral and up a clatterous slope grotesquely sentineled by the night-blackened shapes of motionless saguaros. Past thickets of squatting cedar they tore and up the high arch of a talus-littered hogback which connected this bench with the vast expanse of grease-wood flats surrounding Ryerson's headquarters.

They crested the ridge and the compression of Marratt's knees, together with the savage grip of the yanked-tight reins, set the big roan back on its haunches. Marratt's widened stare held the shock of complete astonishment.

He'd expected to see Ryerson's buildings down there but he hadn't been prepared to see them going up in flames.

Chapter 16

It wasn't the sort of fire which could have caught by itself or have been set off by carelessness. The main house was ablaze from end to end, the big barn was going — the bunkhouse, too. It seemed incredible that anyone should deliberately have intended this; yet he was dealing, Marratt reminded himself, with at least three persons made incalculable by obsessions.

If Crafkin, turned jittery by things he'd not allowed for, had decided the time had come to get rid of Ryerson he might have fired these buildings himself. He might have done it in the hope of drawing Ryerson out of hiding, or be using this means for the disposal of Ryerson's body or to incriminate someone else. He had the greatest opportunity so far as could be figured.

Ryerson also might have set it, or this could have been the work of Gainor whose reasons were not so easily guessed but who obviously had some kind of ax he was bent on sharpening. And there was also that business of Ryerson's safe which, according to Naome, had been smashed open; the smasher may have come back and done this. The Indian Agent could have been back of it.

The place apparently was still deserted. Marratt could see no evidence of human presence.

A great pall of smoke hung over the flat, writhing and twisting in the glow of the flames. The yard down there looked as bright as day and he could see the panicked broncs of the remuda, squealing and pitching in the clutch of terror, as they tore around and around the smoking logs of their enclosure.

No man who loved horses could long watch that, yet Marratt hesitated, bothered by his inability to find any sign of the rider who had traveled this trail just ahead of him. Of course the fellow could be sitting, much as Marratt was himself, a fascinated spectator of the conflagration which must soon reduce those costly buildings to ashes. Just the same, Marratt didn't like it. The man should be in sight if he weren't hiding.

And why should he be hiding? Did he know that Marratt was following him? But that didn't make sense — how could he?

The rider wasn't Naome; she'd have made

straight for those buildings. Unless of course she had been grabbed by somebody lurking in ambush . . .

Marratt snorted. Not even Crafkin could have set that fire in the expectation of getting his hands on Naome. He'd better loose those horses and get the hell out of here before Churk Crafkin *did* come along.

He couldn't think why he should feel so reluctant about going down there. It didn't look like, from here, the flat afforded enough cover in the light of those flames to rig an effective trap even were somebody minded to do it. He tried to rationalize this foreboding and nothing he hit upon could rid his mind of worry. With a disgusted grimace he kneed the big roan forward across the downward sweep of the hogback's arch.

They had not moved ten lengths from the jut of its crest when the trail dropped to a hidden hollow which, now opening up, disclosed a black tangle of mixed oak and sycamore and, above and beyond these, the waiting shape of a motionless horseman.

Marratt, instantly alert, scanned the pooled gloom below the man with lifted hackles. He felt certain that fellow didn't just happen to be posted there.

He wished with bitter anger he'd had the wit to fetch a rifle. But, satisfied at last there was nobody else between them, he said sharply: "Move up, friend. I want to see what you look like."

The man had his legs straight down in the stirrups and he kept them that way, making no move at all. "You'd need a light to do that and if you scratch a match we're done for."

"Mister," Marratt said, "I won't be telling you again."

The man held a hand up like an Indian signaling silence. Then he moved it again, like a cowbird intent on yanking a worm from the ground. Only, this time, its gesture was downward.

Marratt swiveled a look toward the burning buildings. The barn's roof had fallen in and a part of the house roof. There wasn't much left of the bunkhouse and one end of the corral was beginning to take fire. The horses against the far end were plunging like mad but he couldn't pick out any other changes.

The hollow or swale — which in truth it more nearly resembled with its rank growth thrusting ragged tops up out of the darkness — was roughly shaped like a fish hook, about a quarter of a mile long by possibly seventy feet wide at the point where its crescent slashed the path of Marratt's travel. The shank or stem of this depression flanked the left of the hogback while the burning buildings of Ryerson's headquarters were considerably forward and to the right of Marratt's position, with the unidentified horseman just across the hook's curve on high ground directly ahead of him. It was a natural assumption the man's attention was fixed on something which Marratt himself could not see.

Cold slivers of disquiet still scratched at his nerve-ends, but a strengthening curiosity and the plight of those penned-up horses were rapidly fraying the stays of his caution when the man on the point began wickedly to curse.

"What's the rub?" Marratt called.

"Can't you *see* them? It's the girl! That dirty dog of a Crafkin's going to — *Merciful God!*" the man cried and, dragging his rifle, piled out of the saddle.

Even as his shape disappeared in the shadows, Marratt slashed his horse with the knotted reins.

Down into the dank chill of that brush-choked declivity Marratt slammed the big roan with all the power it could muster. He had no thought of traps now, his every faculty was straining to come to grips with Churk Crafkin, to feel the jolting satisfaction of doubled fists pounding flesh. There was a shame in him, too — the shame of having put off for so long a chore which he'd known from the first he'd have eventually to tackle. He should have gone after Crafkin as soon as he'd finished with Tularosa; he had seen the man's danger to Naome right then.

He drove the roan through the brush and between trees hardly seen and was flinging him at the opposite slope, aimed toward where that guy had jumped from the saddle, when the first hint of his folly came racketing out of the swale's leftward bend. That hard rush of horse sound rocketing toward him told him plain as plowed ground how that fellow's slick acting had suckered him into this.

He heard Crafkin's shout above the rataplan thunder of galloping hoofs. Muzzle lights, winking, laced the roaring gloom with the hard clapclapping of high-powered rifles. He whirled his horse off the slope as the now hidden decoy, having gauged the range, commenced a grim search with a pattern of slugs.

Bullets tunneled the shadows, striking trees, clipping branches. Ricochets screamed off the slants of rock surfaces and, throwing a look back across his shoulder, Marratt saw the black shapes of Ryerson's crew tear from cover. He whirled again, spurring the roan toward the ranchward end of the depression's crescent. He didn't need any crystal ball to grasp the full notion of what they were up to, but there wasn't anything he could do about it.

Crafkin hammered his shouts through the din like fists. "Keep him goin'! Keep him goin'!"

Marratt felt no desire to tarry. Not with all that lead whistling round. He was devoting all his energies toward utilizing every last ounce of speed the powerful gelding was able to generate, aware that he was playing into their hands but knowing, too, that nothing save distance could spell survival once they got him lined against the light from those buildings.

And then he felt his horse stumble and the guns slacked off as the hard-hit roan careened round the bend that opened onto the flats. And now he could see them, red as blood in the dying glow of the flames, and he could hear the bleak rasp of the gelding's breathing like the wheeze of a punctured bellows.

He had no choice. He dropped off, landing on skidding bootheels and praying the roan would stay on his feet, at least till those feet carried him out of this ravine.

Not waiting to see, he ran straight at the slope of the hogback's flank, doubled over and spurred to an all-out effort by the ground-shaking rumble of thundering hoofs. It was not too light here but not dark enough for that bunch to miss him without he could get well above eye level.

Twelve feet up he was forced to start climbing and twice he very near started an avalanche when rocks he laid hold of came away in his hands. He made another ten feet of straight-up progress before the Wineglass crew came quirting and spurring round the bulge of the bend. There was nothing he could do then but plaster himself like a fly against that wall and hope like hell there wouldn't none of them look upward.

A sudden shout tore out of that confused mass of riders and Marratt almost lost his grip as shoulder muscles cringed in expectation of impact. But no bullet struck him. No bullet was fired though he heard them pull up in a ragged burst of swearing.

Crafkin's bull-throated bellow flailed into them, furious. "Get after him, you fools! He's on that flat someplace! Get out there and find him!"

The whole bunch churned into motion. But where the ravine debouched onto the open plain they pulled up again and, by their sudden wild uproar, Marratt knew they had sighted the capsized roan.

He dared not wait any longer. With all his back muscles quivering he started climbing again, well knowing the danger in movement but desperately aware, too, of his probable fate should one of that crew happen to glance up and see him. There was no possibility of concealment, no hope of getting beyond range of a bullet so long as he remained on this cliff face. And there were still sixty feet of it between him and the rim.

There seemed to be, however, and just a little way above him, a kind of inverted fold or crevice which he thought, if he could reach it, would facilitate progress immensely. It appeared to bear toward the rim at a decidedly healthier angle than the straight-up contour he was currently encountering.

He was above shale now, on the face of the open stone, finding it increasingly hard to secure hand holds and harder still to find holds for his feet. His whole body ached from the unaccustomed exertion, there was a wheeze in his breathing and he was high enough now that if he fell it would go hard with him.

He did not look toward the fire but he could guess by the amount of light refracted against the cliff that it was about burned out. It was more a red stain than a brightening and fading flicker of flames, but there was still too much of it for him to feel any confidence his shape would not be visible should one of those cursing searchers chance to look in his direction.

He paused to rest a moment, fearing the danger of overtaxing his strength. The nearest portion of the crevice was hardly four feet above his head when, taking new hope from this proximity, he prepared to resume his upward crawl.

He raised his right boot to a new position, tested it cautiously and then, putting weight on it, slid his left hand up to clamp cramping fingers about a bit of rock shelving some eight inches higher. But when he went to pull his left foot onto a new location his gun belt wouldn't let him; it was caught on some kind of projection.

He felt cold sweat creeping out all over him and events long forgotten unreeled irrelevant details across the throbbing screen of his harrowed mind. He tried to pull in his belly but the belt wouldn't budge. He couldn't drop his hips enough to do any good without taking his lifted hand from its hold and working them sideways didn't free the belt, either. But these gyrations, while not helping him, thrust too much of his weight and its accompanying strain on the embedded niggerhead supporting that newly anchored right boot.

He felt the rock give and every screaming nerve telegraphed its panic to a mind already on the brink of desperation.

He did not hear the growled reports of the

disgruntled greasewood beaters or know they had reassembled for further orders where Crafkin sat his chocolate dun hardly a stone's throw away from the wall on which Marratt's belt had so bitterly trapped him. He did not realize the quiet in which they awaited the ramrod's decision. Fright had dug its hooks in him and the roar of his churning emotions turned him blind and deaf to everything but the terrible need for getting instantly off of that loosening boulder.

He didn't think but, acting purely from instinct, dropped his left hand to its former hold, resettled his left foot and his weight along with it and, releasing his right hand, unbuckled the damned belt and let go of it. The gun, sliding free, struck rock — struck again and went off with a blast that ripped the night wide open.

The walls flung back a wild clamor of shouting. Several other guns went off and through this uproar Marratt, not yet discovered, found new grips for his fingers and started rimward again, frantic to get himself into that crevice before one of Crafkin's whippoorwills spotted him.

Had that unseated niggerhead remained in place he might have done so. But no sooner had his lifted foot relinquished its pressure than the boulder tore loose and fell crashing.

Chapter 17

He didn't need Crafkin's shout to know they'd seen him. The sharp *crack-crack* of a fast-firing saddle gun would have told him if the splatter of rock chips and the ricochets hadn't. Discarding the last drag of caution he hauled himself into the water crack barely in time to avoid being riddled in the belated blast from the Wineglass riders.

He didn't stop to catch his breath but shoved everything he had into reaching the rim. What little shelter this crevice afforded was made possible only by the matter of angles which would be no good once that bunch got below him. The upward pitch of the crack — roughly seventy degrees — gave him enough traction to make his efforts count double in the matter of speed.

Even so, his hatless head still lacked five feet of reaching safety when the gunslingers fetched by the Wineglass ramrod started pounding the face of the cliff into rock dust.

The crevice was fogged with this curtain of grit and nothing, it seemed, could survive such a hammering, but poor light and hurry combined to save Marratt's bacon.

He got over the rim.

Teeth on edge and half blinded he crawled away from the racket and dropped flat, exhausted. Blood seeped from a score of shallow wounds cut by rock chips and every muscle, every tendon, quivered with the wrenching strain put on it. But reactions were a luxury Grete Marratt couldn't afford.

He reeled onto his feet, still groggy but knowing how brief was the time he could count on before Crafkin's crew would break out of the shadows hell-bent on finishing the job they had started. Already he could hear the clatter of shod hoofs winging out of that tangle of oak brush and sycamore.

He scrubbed a hand across his jaws and knuckled the sweat from bloodshot eyes. Back away from the rim was the crest of the hogback and scattered thickets of cedar which they'd search straightaway. And back of these the ground dropped through that stand of saguaros into chaparral which was too far away to be of any use to him. Afoot and without any kind of a weapon his only possible chance of escaping destruction was to get back into that swale he'd come out of.

He stumbled toward the steep trail down which the killed roan had taken him, hearing with an alarming increase in loudness the racket of the Wineglass riders coming up it. He thought it must have been Gainor who had fired those buildings but he hadn't any time to pursue that line now.

With Ryerson's headquarters reduced to glowing embers it was much darker up here than it had been. The night swam around him in thick whorls of blackness and, near the head of the trail, he blundered into a rock which knocked the legs out from under him and flung him heavily, gasping, down across its farther side. And none too soon!

Hardly had he hauled his battered body down behind it than Crafkin's crowd came boiling up out of the murk. Creak of leather, clank of metal and the restive stamping of excited panting horses, told Marratt they had stopped short yards away from his concealment.

"He can't of got far," the ramrod's voice abruptly grumbled. "Tracy, you an' Chuck hike along the west flank of this ridge an' keep your eyes peeled. Gimpy an' Gainor will stay here with me in case he tried to double back. Rest of you boys spread out an' comb this hogback an' them cedars off beyond it an' be goddam sure you don't let him get away!"

Marratt sucked in his breath at that mention of Gainor. If the fellow was here with Crafkin it didn't seem too likely he could have had a hand in setting that fire — not at first, that is. But the more he mulled over the implications, the more Marratt was convinced it was exactly what he had done. Listening to the rant of his obsequious whine Marratt could see very plain what that two-faced skunk was up to.

Playing in with Crafkin openly Gainor had spared himself the fate of his more forthright neighbors. He'd been allowed to keep his spread throughout the course of Wineglass expansion. But when Marratt had come into this country and been commonly mistaken for Luke Usher, the man had seen what he considered a good chance to turn the tables.

With what he supposed was Usher's signature on a paper giving him a secret half interest in the patented holdings which the court would be shortly turning over to Luke in compliance with the terms of old Jake's will, Gainor figured he had the whip hand in this deal.

There were plenty of ways he could deal with Luke Usher. What he wanted, of course, was a full scale range war; but whether the supposed Luke gunned Ryerson or not, in the turmoil of such a conflict Gainor could always have both Wineglass principals put out of the way — if he would pay enough for it — knowing the blame would roost right on Luke's doorstep.

Since Luke had failed thus far to become entangled with Wineglass, Gainor had fired Ryerson's buildings to make sure the needed war got properly under way. To anyone familiar with Crafkin's arrogance it was a pretty safe bet that long before this time tomorrow Ryerson's crew, loaded for bear, would be on their way to the Half Circle U.

This was what Gainor was counting on. It was why he had imported that bunch of hired guns which his man had told Marratt to expect in the morning. He had a brand new deck all rigged for slaughter and it was plainly his intention, when the smoke cleared away, to be top dog in this country.

Marratt came out of this thinking to discover they were talking.

"You reckon," Gainor asked, "it was Usher set that fire?"

"You take me for a fool?" Crafkin demanded with a curse.

It was apparent from Gainor's silence he didn't quite know how to take him. Marratt suspected the fat-bellied man was a bit startled and probably nervous besides. If this were so, Crafkin's next words must have just about turned him inside out. Even Marratt's jaw dropped when Ryerson's ramrod said: "That whopperjawed bastard's no more Usher than you are."

"N-Not Usher?"

Had Crafkin been less ingrained in the habit of considering those about him to be either jerks or morons, he must have been struck by the shocked and rageful cadence of a voice which had for once forgotten to employ its unctuous whine.

But if the ramrod noticed he gave no sign of having done so. Hauling up burly shoulders he spat and said as one scattering his pearls before swine, "If Luke Usher had run into what this guy did that first night he'd have been gone before sun-up. Luke — the *real* Luke — never had the kind of nerve that goes with the things this bird has been pulling. Moreover Krantz came out from the Red Horse, just before you rode up, with a sample of this jasper's signature; he spells it the same but it ain't Luke's writing. Luke Usher's hair wasn't sandy. It was the color of his guts and —"

"Churk! You up there, Churk?"

"Ryerson," Crafkin muttered; and the hidden man saw his short and broad shape wheel its horse toward the rim to call, "Yes, sir. You had better come up."

Marratt didn't wait to hear anything further. He knew if he were ever to get away from here alive, now was the time to make his try while the sounds of Ryerson's approach could help to cover his departure.

He slipped off his spurs and left them, moving cautiously down the ink-black slope, the progress of Ryerson's climbing horse serving to keep him headed in the right direction. Once he tripped and came within an ace of stumbling but met and passed the Wineglass owner without discovery. It made his neck hair bristle to see the vague outline of Clagg's partner within six feet of him and, despite his ultimatums, not be able to raise a hand. A more religiously inclined person might have taken it as a sign, but Marratt's thoughts at the moment were a considerable way from heaven. He had got to thinking, crazily, about that mongrelly pup turning up again . . .

His ears began to ache with the strain of listening and it was hard to be careful when you had to test your footing for every stride before you took it. He longed to run like a deer but he continued his snail-like advance toward the place where the hollow's crescent gave onto the open flats facing Wineglass, sometimes creeping and crawling where the brush made progress difficult. And in the end it paid off.

He found out he wasn't alone when an unseen thorny branch, raking him painfully across the face, dragged a curse from his throat and a challenging *"Quien es?"* jumped out of the darkness ahead of him.

Cold sweat beaded Marratt's cheeks as flame leaped out of the same place and gun sound belted the walls with its clamor. He was on hands and knees and the lead went whistling over him but he'd have been a cooked goose if he had been on his feet.

Crafkin's voice roared angrily down from the rim and the man who had fired said he'd thought he'd heard something. "Thought?" Crafkin snarled. "You ain't got the equipment! You do what you're told and leave the thinking to me!" And then three more shots banged out and there were shouts made thin by distance and a racket of hoofs told the ground-hugging Marratt Crafkin's group had left the rim.

While the echoes were still slamming sound through the hollow he went forward in a catfooting crouch until he saw the head and shoulders of the Wineglass *vaquero* against the distant shine of stars. The man was mounted, staring upward, obviously absorbed with the receding commotion above.

Then, before Marratt could gain a position from which a leap would hold out any chance of success, the man's chin came down and he got out of the saddle.

Marratt could not see him now but he could see the saddled back of the man's horse coming toward him. The animal sensed his presence and, suddenly planting its feet, set back on the reins and would not come any nearer. The man growled a curse in Spanish and abruptly went still as though listening and staring. Marratt kept still, too, hardly daring to breathe, until he heard the man start to back off with his horse; then he lunged for him.

The man's shoulder hooked him hard in the chest. The horse snorted and Marratt slugged the man with a rock-weighted fist and grabbed the reins from his hand as the fellow went down. The horse tried to jerk free but Marratt dug in his heels. When the horse quit fighting Marratt swiftly stooped and got the man's gun and shell belt, buckled the latter around him and, catching up the fellow's chin-strapped sombrero, thrust a foot in the stirrup and swung aboard.

Seldom had he experienced such a beautiful feeling; but there was too much at stake for any carelessness now and he held the horse down to a moderate walk until he was absolutely certain Crafkin's crowd could not hear them.

★ ★ ★

The first gray pallor of false dawn was in the air when Marratt's appropriated Wineglass gelding brought him, via Jake's south forty, into sight of the dilapidated Usher headquarters. The dark huddle of buildings showed no glimmer of light. Nor could he observe any sign of human presence though, from the corrals, a horse nickered and the bronc he was forking gave tired reply. Kid Boots, of the saturnine eyes and fast pistol, was being awfully damned quiet. Playing cagey, Marratt imagined until he recalled the inclination of Indian curs toward barking.

He remembered then with an irascible dissatisfaction several other things; the way Boots had targeted that strap iron hasp and the quietness with which he'd put his things in Jake's bedroom. A really smart man would have been a little more careful. He'd not have lied about the dog which Boots had said looked to him like anyone's pooch that would call it. Sure enough, he had come straightaway to Marratt's whistle; but he hadn't that first time. He hadn't come at the tank when the girl had asked, "*What* dog!" And there were Crafkin's remarks to clinch it.

He turned the Wineglass bronc toward the nearest of the pole enclosures and swung down when he reached it for a look through the bars. The hired man's horse was there but the uncut gray he'd got from Isham was gone.

He dropped the reins and turned around and rummaged the yard with a probing stare. Common sense told him he was acting like a fool. He didn't see anything to get his hackles up. Far away to the south a coyote's yammer made a solitary sound in the immensity of space, and the forlornness of it seemed immeasurably to emphasize the untenable bleakness of Marratt's position. But the fellow was gone or that dog would be barking.

The prod of frayed nerves promptly jeered at such logic. The pup could be trained to keep still . . .

Marratt, silently cursing, moved across the gray gloom. Partway to the back door he swung left on a hunch around the side of the house, impelled by something stronger than reason to have another look at that front porch.

But again the cold jitters inside him howled protest and his feet slowed and stopped in the sound-muffling grass thirty feet from the edge of its weather-warped planks.

"Come on. Don't stop there." The voice, smoothly ominous, came out of the shadows where he'd left Boots sitting. Only it wasn't Boots' voice.

Chapter 18

It was a voice he'd never heard before, and it directed implacably: "Move up. Move up or you're a dead duck, hombre."

Marratt, in extreme disgust, scanned his chances and growled resignedly, "All right." There was no percentage in trying to beat the drop of an unseen firearm and the man's hands held one or he'd have played this different. "Keep your shirt on," Marratt grumbled, and stepped bitterly forward until the voice bade, "Far enough. Now turn around and shuck that gun belt."

This wasn't Crafkin. It wasn't Gainor, though it might very well be one of the latter's imported slugslammers. An angry urge rushed through Marratt to spin and grab, gunfighter fashion; but while he'd frequently been foolish he was not a fool.

He did as he'd been told and, when the gun-weighted belt hit the ground, his captor ordered, "Strike a match, mount the steps and go inside and get a lamp lit."

"Would you mind," Marratt asked, "telling me what you think you're about to do?"

"We'll get to that. Meantime just remember if you drop that match, or if it should happen to go out, you're going to pass out right along with it. Get up here now and step lively."

Because he hadn't much choice Marratt, rasping a match across the hip of his Levis, climbed onto the porch and moved into the house. He found the lamp, dragged flame over the wick and replaced the chimney. He didn't hear the man follow but, when he turned, there he was, spare and florid in a pair of wool socks.

It wasn't the gun which caught Marratt's stare but the bright flash of metal on the pocket of his shirt. That, and the triangular eyes above it so balefully filled with a beady satisfaction.

"A real pleasure, Mister Usher," declared Bella Loma's marshal, a mocking grin pulling back the leathery lips from mossy teeth. "That Mex headgear nearly throwed me but, like I always say, you don't have to be right to be President. Jump first —"

"All right," Marratt said, "you've jumped. What's the next move?"

"Jail for you, boy; an' my advice to you is

make a clean breast of everything. Tell the truth an' shame the devil, as my mother used to say. If you've got what these shysters call —"

"I think you've treed the wrong coon, Hanna."

"It don't cost nothin' to think. But I'll tell you right now that kinda talk ain't going to help you. I been marshalin' towns for the past twenty years an' never once saw no guy, wrapped up like you are, beat the rope without help."

Marratt, with no means of knowing what was in the marshal's craw but imagining the man had got onto his identity, said: "What's the price of your help and what will it amount to?"

"Now you're talkin' my language," the marshal nodded. "A man's got to look out for Number One in this world. So here's the way we'll do it. On receipt of your signed confession an' a bonafide quitclaim deed to this spread I'll put the chance in your way to make a run for the border."

"And if the confession and deed aren't forthcoming?"

"You don't look," Hanna said, "like a guy that would very much enjoy a hemp necktie. Let's cut out the bull. You got a pen an' some paper?"

Behind inscrutable cheeks Grete Marratt was finding this mighty queer talk. The man must still think him Usher and, if he did, this was a frame. But if it was that fire they were fixing to charge him with, why this talk about hanging? Had Gainor accused him of killing Luke's father?

Hanna said, "Well — what you waitin' on?"

"I was trying to figure out what I'm supposed to confess to."

"Beckwith's killin', of course. You needn't put on with me."

"I didn't kill Beckwith —"

"Makes no difference to me if you did or you didn't. You're goin' to hang for it, boy, if you don't write me them papers. You went down there two days ago an' had a row with the feller. Now he turns up dead in his office which looks like a cyclone went through it, an' your hat's on the floor. On top of that you put a check that come out of Beckwith's files —"

"That's not proof —"

"It's a jury you got to convince, not me." Hanna picked up the gun belt he'd fetched in from outside and broke open the pistol he pulled from its holster. "One shot fired. One chunk of lead the doc dug out of Beckwith. An' you think any jury's goin' to listen to you?"

"It won't come to no jury," Kid Boots

drawled from the doorway. "You won't, either, without you drop them guns pronto."

There was a ludicrous look on the marshal's face. "Pick 'em up, boss," Kid Boots said, and Marratt lifted the guns from Ives Hanna's lax fingers.

The marshal came to life then. "You're makin' a mistake —"

"It won't be the first," said Kid Boots, unconcerned. His green eyes grinned derisively. "You want I should knock off this sidewinder now or —"

"I think," Marratt said, "we'd better tie him up. I'll keep him covered. Get the rope off your saddle —"

"You can't get away with this!" Hanna shouted. He glared at them wildly, a man clearly beside himself with rage and balked greed. "I'll hunt you two down if —"

"You won't have to hunt far then. We're not going anyplace," Marratt told him — "not before Churk Crafkin and your sidekick, Ryerson, have paid up for the misery they've caused on this range. Get that rope, Boots."

While the man was gone Marratt, ignoring the marshal's bluster and ranting, sat watching him with thoughts that seemed to have flown well beyond the confines of this room. At last he said, cutting into the lawman's invective, "You're wasting your breath. There's

213

a new day in store for this Bella Loma country and it's time you took a long look at your hole card. Some time this morning there's apt to be quite a ruckus here and if you want to try dealing from the top for a change I might give you the same chance you just offered me. The chance to get across the border when the pay-off comes."

Hanna told him what he could do with it, and when Kid Boots came back with the rope Marratt said, "I guess you better swear me in as a special deputy."

"I can see myself!"

Marratt nodded to Kid Boots. "See what a few swipes with that pistol will do."

"Hey! Wait! Hold on; you can't — I'll do it," gulped the marshal, hurriedly capitulating when the yellow-haired man, grinning, spat on his gun barrel. "I'll do it, but we got to have a —"

"Bible?" asked Boots, and produced one from a dusty stack of books piled behind a horsehair rocker. When the ceremony was over Marratt, unpinning Hanna's badge, refastened it to his own shirt and, considering the marshal sadly, told Kid Boots to tie and gag him.

"Now," said Marratt, when this had been accomplished, "take him out to the barn and drop him in a feed rack and pull enough hay down to make sure he won't be noticed. Time you get back I'll have breakfast ready."

And he just about did.

While they were lighting smokes and sitting back with third cups of coffee, Marratt said: "Where were you last night when Hanna came touring onto the place? And don't bother thinking up any tall stories. Just give me the truth, Usher, and give it to me straight."

The green eyes gleamed and Kid Boots showed his crooked teeth, but he said, apparently more relieved than bothered about it, "How did you catch on?"

"I wasn't sure," Marratt answered, "until you dug up that Bible, but I was pretty well convinced when I overheard Crafkin telling Gainor I wasn't Usher. He said the real Luke had yellow hair, or words to that effect."

"I can imagine," Usher nodded, "the words that bird would use to describe me. What other slips did I make?"

"You should never have turned up with that dog. I had already seen him on the reservation; I knew he wasn't anyone's dog that would call him because I'd already tried. I got to wondering what you'd been doing around Beckwith's office, and why you'd bother to deny ownership of a dog that was obviously yours. I was bound to conclude you didn't want me to know you'd been over there."

"But that didn't tell you I was Luke Usher."

"No, but it made a couple of other things seem a lot more significant. I knew the real Luke Usher was considered fast with a gun. When I told you to demonstrate on that strap iron hasp, the way you drew and fired without hardly looking showed you knew more about it than any stranger would be likely to. You smacked it first crack but when I asked you to repeat you deliberately missed it, proving you'd seen the error of having hit it the first time. You were hoping I would pass that shot off as luck. All and all, you see, you were giving me quite a bit to think about. Your next mistake, much worse than all the others, was in putting your belongings where I'd told you in Jake's bedroom. No one unfamiliar with the house would have known where that was, or that the bedroom you went into had been Jake's rather than Luke's. You didn't hunt around. You went straight to it, left your stuff, and came out again."

"Still the fool," Usher grunted. "How come you didn't slug me?"

"Same reason, I suppose, you haven't ventilated me. Wanted to see what you were up to."

Usher's lips pulled back in a twisted grin. "I

wasn't being crowded like you are, Marratt."

In his chair Marratt's shape went uncomfortably still. "So you know who I am."

"I've seen the reward bills; they don't half do you justice, no idea of your coloring, your real personality. I was over in the barn the night Frailey brought you in. I took a squint after he left. You look more like Jake's son than I do. Did you kill that damn agent?"

"No." Marratt said, "Did you kill Jake?"

Usher came half out of his chair, eyes like gun steel. Then a sick, shamed expression writhed through them and he shook his head, hating himself. "If I'd had any guts I'd have evened the score, though. I'd ridden into the yard, had just got off my horse when I heard the shot. I ran around the house. Dad was down on the ground, Ryerson standing over him with a smoking pistol. I saw Crafkin gettin' set to crack down on me." His eyes filled with an indescribable anguish. "I cut my stick — turned tail and bolted like a goddam rabbit!"

"I've been tempted to bolt a few times myself —"

"But this wasn't your fight. Why should you stick your neck out?"

"It's more my fight than you'd be likely to guess. If you've seen the reward bills you know why they sent me to Yuma."

"I've wondered about that. Read a little,

217

back along, in the papers. Figured maybe you was framed —"

"No, I killed him. There were two of them . . . and a girl. Ryerson was Clagg's partner."

"So that was why you took up my quarrel —"

"No," Marratt said, "I'll not fool you. I didn't know when I stepped into your boots what his name was, or that I'd find him in this country. I broke jail to find him and I had to stay clear long enough to get a line on him. The guy in the Lone Star called me Luke; and then Frailey, making the same mistake, supplied a little of your background. I saw a chance to keep the law off my neck."

"You took a damn long chance —"

"But it payed off," Marratt nodded. "Frailey introduced me to Naome and, while we were talking, Ryerson came up —"

"He wouldn't rest after that, not with you free to call him. Why didn't you drop him right then?"

"He didn't have a gun on him —"

"Neither did my Dad; though they said afterwards he had." Usher got up, tramping round the room restively. "What are we going to do?"

"I don't think —"

"Don't count me out of this. I'm through with running!"

Marratt gave him a searching scrutiny. "All right. You'll need to understand what I've discovered, what's happening." He roughed it in for him, concluding gruffly, "So you can see the whole thing is going to come to a boil right here on this spread within the next three-four hours. It's not going to be any Sunday school picnic."

Usher said grimly, "I didn't come back figurin' it was going to be easy." He stopped across from Marratt and stood a moment, scowlingly silent. He dug out a four-bits piece. "You want to toss for Ryerson?"

"There's a chance," Marratt said, "he never killed old Jake —"

"He kep' his mouth shut, didn't he?"

Marratt said with an air of discovering something: "That isn't quite the same." Then, flushed and resentful of the embarrassment occasioned by Usher's sharp look, he growled, "Not that I'm wanting to defend him. But fear can play hell with any man's thinking and, for whatever it's worth, I feel bound to tell you Frailey doesn't believe Ryerson killed your father."

Usher said gruffly, "You're lettin' that girl run away with your judgment. I know what I saw —"

He broke off, reaching for his gun as, green eyes bleak, he jumped for the door.

Chapter 19

Though still dark and with the tatters of night blackly piled in the hollows and wreathed like widows' veils about the lost shapes of trees, dawn was definitely on the upswing when Ryerson's range boss finally quit and called his crew off the hunt. He found it hard to believe the pseudo Usher had escaped him yet the man very obviously had.

Nor was Crafkin's frame of mind at all improved when the Mexican left in the ravine turned up missing. Neither Galardo nor his horse responded to Crafkin's cursing; and hard on the heels of this he made a further, more jolting discovery when a swift count of noses revealed that Ryerson, too, had hauled his freight.

"Probably back at the ranch," offered Gainor; but a subsequent search of the gutted Wineglass headquarters failed completely to yield any sign of the ranch owner's whereabouts.

The last lingering of shadows were pretty well scattered by that time. "The old woman," said Gainor, elaborately yawning and stretching, "will be thinkin' I've fell in a boghole. I reckon, Churk, I better be gettin' along home."

It was like a spark hitting powder the way Crafkin whirled on him, catching Gainor's shirtfront in a grip of steel. "You ain't wrigglin' out of my sight till I say so! If that guy wants fire we'll give him fire, an' when I get done there won't nobody else ever dare stand against me!"

"Hell, man, I'm for it," bleated Gainor with his cheeks suddenly quivering, "but you won't be needin' *me* —"

"I'll be needin' all my friends."

"But what could *I* do?" Gainor quavered, his desperation close to panic as he thought of the trap he'd ordered rigged for this guy's welcome. "You know I'm no good for that kind of thing. Can't hit a barn door — can't stand the sound of —"

"You can sit a horse, by God, an' you'll be sittin one today when we ride in to settle accounts with that Paul Pry that calls himself Usher!"

"Horse comin'," Luke said tersely, with a narrowed eye squinting out through the door crack; and then, with less tolerance: "Ryerson's daughter."

"Where's the dog?" Marratt asked.

"Tied him up in the barn to keep him clear of blue whistlers. You want him?"

Marratt stood undecided a moment, seemingly weighing the merits of some considered course of action and looking none too pleased with the results of this cogitation. They heard the saddle creak as the girl swung down, heard her crossing the porch. "Let her in," Marratt said, and Luke pulled open the door.

She was still in her squaw boots and buckskin and her dark eyes, wide and round, found Marratt's face and clung to it; and she put out her hands. "Is Dad all right?"

Marratt nodded. "I left him riding with the crew."

Relief swept through her glance then it got dark again with worry and with something which caused Usher, noticing, to go out, quietly pulling the door shut behind him.

Marratt, seeing too, crucified by his thoughts and by the unwanted remembrance of Frailey's parting words, stood for what seemed an eternity without speaking. *That girl*, Frailey'd said, *is in love with you;* and the truth of this statement lay plain and afraid in the eyes searching his.

"I thought," he said harshly, "you were staying in town."

"But I couldn't." She put a lifted hand against her left breast. "I had a terrible feeling — like a knife twisting in me; and then I realized what Crafkin would do when he learned —"

"I'm man grown, Naome."

"But it won't be just him. He'll throw the whole weight of Wineglass against you! What chance will you have? Oh, Luke . . . I couldn't bear —"

"Naome, I must tell you I am not Luke Usher. I'm —"

She put a hand across his mouth. "As if that could matter so long as —"

"But it does . . . it matters terribly. I —" He squared his shoulders. "I'm Grete Marratt."

No look of shock went through her, no dawning horror turned away her eyes. They continued — filled unbearably with trust and love, with all the things she was offering — to gaze deep into his own tortured gray ones. The name meant nothing at all to her.

"I'm a convict." He swallowed hard. "A killer escaped from Yuma!"

"What does that change?"

Marratt broke. He pulled her to him with a kind of sob; and as they clung together the porch door was shoved open and Luke's

223

twisted face said: "They're comin'! Get her out of there!"

Marratt, stumbling off the porch, caught the reins of her horse from Luke's clenched hand. He saw the dust, like smoke, boiling over the trees that obscured the road.

Luke's hand grabbed his shoulder. "What's she waitin' on?"

"She's staying —"

"Stayin'!" Luke's eyes blazed. "An' you're *lettin'* her?"

Marratt squeezed the sweat off his bearded cheeks.

With an outraged expression Usher drew back a fist, then with a snarl let it fall. "Why don't you get the hell out of this country?"

Marratt shook his head. "There are things a man has to do in this world —"

"Like killin' a fine sweet girl off by inches? Damn you, Marratt! If you got one grain of decency —"

"I'm seeing this through." He drew Naome's rifle from beneath the stirrup fender and his jaw was like granite. He thrust the black's reins at Usher. "Take the horse in the house and keep out of sight." He shoved him roughly. "Get in there and keep me covered!"

Wheeling then, with the rifle loose-slanting from the crook of an elbow, he took a few careless strides in the direction of the men riding into the yard and stopped, implacably waiting for Gainor's bunch to come up.

They were five, varying in the details of their physical appearance but cut to a pattern; bleak hard-eyed men with the gunsmoke smell saturating their clothing along with the sweat and steamy pungence of horseflesh.

They hauled their mounts up before him in a loose half-circle, the small and dark man who had accosted him in town allowing lean shaved lips to curl with an obvious amusement.

"Mornin' . . . boss. My name is Green and this is your crew, delivered as advertised. You want to say a few words before the boys go to work?"

"Might save them a little grief," Marratt nodded. "You fellows were hired by Clint Gainor to come over here this morning and, in the guise of being this spread's paid employees, to blast hell out of Wineglass. I think you ought to know before you start burning powder Gainor slipped a couple of cogs in sizing up this situation."

Green's eyes were still amused. "I guess the size of this crew will take up any slack."

"The mistakes Gainor made could get you boys in a lot of trouble. In the first place Gainor's orders were given on the erroneous assumption he had acquired a half interest in this ranch. At the point of a gun he got me to give him a paper to that effect which doesn't happen to be worth the time it took to write it."

"How do you get hold of that notion?"

"Gainor's paper is worthless," Marratt said, "because the man who owns this property never so much as saw it."

"What kind of guff you tryin' to hand us?"

"If he takes it to court I'll prove that signature's a forgery."

"You made it," Green said skeptically.

"But it happens I'm not Luke Usher." Marratt's smile loosed the gleam of hard white teeth. "You boys might as well turn around and ride home."

There was no amusement in Green's stare now. He said, softly wicked, "Who the blue blazes *are* you?"

"The name is Grete Marratt and for this day, at least, I'm packin' just about all the law there is in these parts. As special deputy," he drawled, tapping Hanna's badge with the back of a thumbnail, "you might say I've been sent in here to iron out this trouble."

Green's eyes considered him narrowly. "What about Ives Hanna?"

"My warrant exceeds Mr. Hanna's authority. I'll have to write you boys down as trespassers. Of course, if you want to ride out —"

"We're stickin'," Green said.

"Then you're taking my orders!"

"Let's hear 'em."

Marratt, hiding his frustration behind inscrutable cheeks, said, "Take your horses over back of those trees to the left and tie them there somewhere where they'll not be seen."

Green hoisted a leg across the horn and swung down. The rest followed suit. Flicking a nod at one of the others the dark man grunted, "That's a job for you, Curly," and the man so-selected started their mounts toward the trees.

Too late Marratt discovered that, in sliding from their saddles, Gainor's crew had so maneuvered things he was now caught fast between them.

"I guess you're through with giving orders for awhile," Green jeered; and something hard crashed down across the top of Marratt's head.

Crafkin, riding in the van of a handpicked Wineglass crew, had no reason to believe he'd any need of such a force to put this pseudo Usher where cold weather wouldn't bother him. But he was all done taking chances. He meant to catch him dead to rights and snuff his light for sure this time.

In all their previous encounters the man had appeared to be playing a lone hand. He probably still was; but if he'd smuggled in some help or enlisted aid in the vicinity, the twelve men Crafkin was fetching to this chore should prove ample to get the job done. Then he would tend to Ryerson and that slick piece of baggage Ryerson's squaw had whelped.

He wasn't anticipating any trouble but, this time, he was allowing for it. He stopped the crew two miles west of Usher's headquarters and, splitting the bunch into two groups, told Gainor: "You'll take these five and ride straight in. He may not be there, but if he is he'll see you comin' and fort-up in the house or the barn, most likely. Your job's to smoke him out of there. I'll take the rest and come up through the trees. That way, no matter what he does, we'll have him. Understand?"

Gainor, green about the gills, looked ready to collapse. He had to try three times before his tongue could scrape up enough moisture for sound, and even then it was more like the skreak of a gate hinge. "Wh-Wh-What if he's g-got help?"

"An' where would he be gettin' help around here?" Crafkin grinned derisively. "You talk like a guy that hasn't got all his buttons. Pull yourself together! An' just remember, Mister Gainor, if you try to pull a bolt and slope, these boys has got orders to drop you."

Green deployed his crew with the aplomb of a master strategist. Not guessing there was anybody hidden in the house, and assuming it would draw the bulk of Crafkin's fire-power, he kept his bunch away from it. One man he bedded beneath the sun-curled slats of a rickety wagon that was falling apart across the yard from the barn. Another was sent into the saddle shed which flanked the same side of the house as the wagon. A third took up his stand in the bunkhouse and the last he fetched into the barn with himself.

"Let them get right into the yard," he called, "then give it to 'em proper."

From the house Usher, hugging his rifle, had seen and heard everything which had happened in the yard. When he saw how Marratt was trapped by the way Green's bunch had got out of their saddles, his jaws locked hard against the accusing outraged look flung his way by the girl who was crouched just across the room from him. But he didn't let her words stampede him into firing. Not even when Marratt suddenly folded and pitched groundward under the bludgeoning impact of a swung pistol barrel did Luke put finger to trigger.

"You despicable coward!" Naome lashed at him fiercely, and would have snatched the Colt's .45 from his holster had he not slapped her hand away and, whirling, roughly grabbed her.

"You tryin' to get him killed? Then don't be a fool!" he growled. "He knew what chance he was taking when he went out there —"

"He told you to cover him. I heard him. Let me go!" she cried, her voice choked with anger. "Take your hands off me!"

"I will when you show enough sense to behave. He's got a chance so long as they don't know we're here. They'll tie him up and dump him out of sight someplace till they get done with what they came to do —"

"They came to kill him!"

"On the contrary." Luke said with tired patience, "They came here on Gainor's orders to blast hell out of Crafkin's outfit which, by the simple expedient of last night burning all your dad's fancy buildings, Gainor —"

"He burned Wineglass?"

"Sure, but he made Crafkin think it was Marratt that did it. So now Crafkin's hog-wild to stop Marratt's clock. He'll be showin' up with all the toughs he can gather. Soon as the guns start to crackin' — if you'll promise to do as I tell you — I'll slip out and get Marratt loose."

She didn't reply right away but she quit struggling. After a moment he let her go and stepped back, being careful to stay out of line with the window.

"Who is he?" she asked.

"Who you talkin' about now?"

"Luke — I mean Marratt."

"He's a guy with one chip in a no-limit game. Hold my rifle," he growled and, when she took it, went off through the hall, coming back with an armful of pillows and bedclothes which he dropped on the sofa. There was an extra shell belt and pistol strapped about his lean hips now.

"They've carried him into the barn," Naome whispered.

"What I figured." He took back his rifle. "You can help us both by gettin' down on that sofa. Wad all that stuff I brought between you and the back of it; this is like to be rough when that lead gets to flyin'. An' while —"

"But if he's not Jake's son why would he let people think he is? And why," she asked desperately, "would he be carrying on Luke's crazy feud with my father?"

"He ain't."

She looked up at him queerly. "But he said —"

"I can't help that. The trouble between him and your old man hasn't anything to do with this ranch. Nor with its owners."

Something about his way of saying that caught at her notice and she looked at him oddly, searching his face with a kind of baffled wonder. And then, again taken up in her own worries: "Do you suppose Dad would possibly decide to ride over here with Crafkin?"

"Not a chance! He's too —" Usher broke it off, listening. "They're coming," he said. "Get onto that sofa and don't budge an inch till I get back here with Marratt!"

Chapter 20

It was the pounding of the guns which battered Marratt back to consciousness. He imagined the tumultuous crash-crashing must take the top of his head off surely; and then the black rage that was bottled inside him began to make itself manifest, clawing his shuddering mind from its hiding. He opened his eyes and the cares of the past became again present problems.

He'd been dumped on the floor of a cobwebby box stall, trussed like a plucked fowl ready for the basting. From the bend of their knees his legs were drawn taut behind him with a length of rope passed around his windpipe. The least pressure on this arrangement fetched excruciating pain. To prevent any chance of an outcry he'd been gagged. Green had been thorough. He had had Marratt's wrists yanked around behind him and securely lashed across the arch of his insteps. There was no possibility of

Marratt freeing himself.

The gun racket which had roused him seemed about to have spent itself and was now dwindled away to the random noise of snipers. A man's voice near the front of the barn said jubilantly, "Reckon that about does her, Gus — ain't a one of that bunch even wrigglin'."

Green's voice, nearer Marratt, cautioned, "Stay where you are. Don't go out in that yard yet."

"Hell! There ain't none of them fellers playin' possum."

"You don't know that. Give the sun a quarter hour to get in its licks then we'll go and have a look at 'em."

In his need to get loose Marratt thought of the dog which, according to Usher, had been tied up in this barn. But he couldn't hear any sound of it, not even the stertorous sound of its panting.

As though great minds were frequenting the same channel, the fellow up front said, " 'F you hadn't bashed that dog's head in we could send him out there."

Green merely grunted.

Time commenced most abominably to drag.

Marratt's mouth, parched and miserable with the gag they'd crammed in it, longed for water. His whole racked body cried out for it and a pair of buzzing flies, playing tag through the dust motes, abruptly settled on his face and commenced to crawl over it, pausing now and then to lick a leg or scrape a whisker.

Marratt presently got the feeling there was somebody watching him. It bothered him almost as much as the flies did, and he wondered if it were Green making up his mind what to do with him. No matter what role Gainor's scheming had assigned him they had no real reason for keeping him alive now. They could knock him off any time and be rid of the risk his tongue represented. It was their obvious course now they'd got rid of Crafkin.

Green could pin on Hanna's badge and tell any tale he wanted; always providing, of course, they'd found and liquidated Hanna. Or he could leave it where it was and spin a mighty fancy story of how Usher, saying his name was Marratt and calling himself the law in these parts, had deputized Green's outfit, ordering them to wipe out the Wineglass invaders. He could say Usher, unfortunately, had been killed in the fighting, and show his dead body to prove it.

Who would call him a liar? Not Ryerson or Gainor.

There was Naome, of course, and Luke — the real Usher; but Marratt wasn't pinning any shining hope on that lad. Luke had run out once and had probably sloped again. Or, if he'd fired on this bunch when that gun barrel had knocked Marratt loose of his intentions, he was probably dead — and the girl along with him. For Gainor, no less than Churk Crafkin, had been playing a desperate game here of late and would be extremely unlikely to let the life of any woman stand between himself and the spoils he was after.

Green said, "Give it five more minutes an' we'll go strip off those masks and see what kind of ducks you boys potted."

"Reckon Crafkin was with 'em?"

"Clint aimed to make sure of that. Said he figured the Big Mogul would likely be along, too."

"Crew seemed kinda light. I'd of thought he'd have fetched his whole crowd in for this trick."

"No reason why he should. He wasn't lookin' to find anyone here but Luke Usher —"

"Gus!" the man up front cried excitedly. "Git up here an' grab a eyeful of this!"

Marratt heard somebody high-heel it doorward. Green's low voice rasped furiously, "Where the hell did *she* come from?"

"Come outa the house," the other guy said; and abruptly Grete Marratt had something else on his mind.

A sharp knife had slashed the rope passed round his neck and was severing the knotted turns wrapped about his wrists and ankles. Feeling churned through him in nauseous waves as cramped limbs fell free and released blood roared through his near atrophied arteries. Sweat broke coldly out of his body. Bursts of light warped his vision laced with fragments of blackness and the sides of the stall rocked about him like planks in the grip of a raging sea.

Then his eyes swam back to a normal focus. Surrounding sounds were picked up and Usher's face, thrust close to his own, admonished, "They're still here. Take it easy."

He felt Usher massaging the numbness from legs and ankles and he commenced awkwardly chafing pins and needles into the corrugations of his lacerated wrists. He heard Green say: "She's headin' straight for us!" And Green's trigger-tripper said, "I ain't never had no Inj—"

"Christ a'mighty!" Green roared. "Let her in and get that door shut —"

Whatever else Green may have said was lost in a sudden wild banging of Winchesters. Crafkin's bull-throated shout rolled out of the trees and off somewhere in the direction of the harness shed one man's yell climbed higher than hearing. Lead hammered the front and left sides of the barn and two slugs, tearing through, kicked twin boards off the far wall's studding, letting in bright oblongs of the outside glare.

"Crafkin played it foxy," Usher muttered with his mouth almost brushing Marratt's ear — "biggest half of his bunch are in them box elders and Green's already give his hand away. Here —" He shoved the extra belt and gun he had fetched into Marratt's still awkward fingers.

Buckling the leather about his waist, Marratt tried the weapon for heft and reeled out of the stall without bothering to learn whether Usher was following. He directed his shambling pace toward the front where he could see Green crouched behind the not-quite-shut door coolly waiting for something to throw down on.

Green's companion was stuffing fresh cartridges into a rifle some twelve strides to Green's right where a broken-out piece of the rotten planking provided a circumscribed view of the yard. Naome lay midway between the two Gainor men, uncaringly sprawled on the straw littered floor where a bullet or one of their fists had dropped her.

Sight of that pitifully still, disheveled shape did something to Marratt. A monstrous rage beat and tore at him as his jerked-away stare settled wickedly on Green; and he went lurching toward him, the racket of the guns obscuring any sound kicked up by his advance.

Green's bent back made a slight turn in shifting as he tried for a clearer look at something outside; Green's man yelled "Gus —" and died, still whirling, in the blast from Usher's pistol.

Green's head twisted around and wide-sprung eyes, peering over his shoulder, caught Marratt in their focus. He tried to bring up his gun, pivoting as he did so, a touch of craziness in the grin that showed his broken teeth. His gun and Marratt's spoke almost in unison, the breath of that slug fanning Marratt's shirt. But Green was all done with breathing. He was down on his back with no more use for a pistol.

Marratt tore it out of the man's lax fingers and with a gun in each fist heard Luke cry, "Wait —" but he was through with waiting. Naome also lifted a yell at him but, pausing only to accustom his eyes to the glare, he stepped full into the smash of the sun.

The yard was a shambles. The only one of Green's men still working a trigger was forted-up in the bunkhouse and, even as Marratt moved into the open, this one's rifle quit barking.

Crafkin, with three of his Wineglass crew,

catapulted from cover in a dive for the bunkhouse, unconscious of Marratt's appearance behind them, bent on nailing Gainor's man before the fellow could reload. Marratt, hurrying after them, was partway across the barn's broad front when Usher's voice, coming around its far side through the forty-foot alley between barn and bunkhouse, called: "Rack up the balls, boys."

It stopped Crafkin's crew like a rope stretched before them.

But only for a moment. Ryerson's range boss, bellowing, flung his shape to one side and chopped down with his belt gun, firing from the hip. A man beside him, caught in the blast from Luke's rifle, doubled over; another spun and pitched headlong. "Hold it!" Marratt yelled; but Crafkin, whirling, loosed every bean he had in the cylinder.

The shell belt was torn from about Marratt's middle. Something hammered his chest and he went staggering backward, feeling his legs suddenly folding up under him. He felt grass against his duststreaked face. He pushed his chest off the ground, got an elbow braced under him and finally, carefully, squeezed out two shots at Crafkin and saw the Wineglass ramrod go down.

Chapter 21

Luke, propped up under Frailey's care on
Jake's front-room sofa and still swathed in
bandages five days after the Green-Crafkin
battle, declared irritably, "And I tell you
again I don't know *where* he is!"

Naome's eyes searched his face. "Did you
give him my notes?"

" 'Course I never give 'em to him — how
the hell *could* I? Like I keep tryin' to tell you,
right after you lit out for town to fetch Frailey
he saddled up that big gray studhorse he
brought an' took off, headin' south."

"But he was in no condition to ride!"

"I won't argue about that. All I know is he
rode. An' he sure didn't waste no time gettin'
started."

"But why?" she asked despairingly. "Why
would he ride off like that without a word?"

Luke, who had advocated this very course
of action, didn't believe there was anything
else Marratt could have done, feeling the way

he did about the girl. Luke privately considered him one of the whitest men he'd known but this did not alter the fact of his being a killer, a man convicted of what amounted to murder and sentenced to Yuma for the rest of his natural. No, the clean break was best and swiftest mended.

"I reckon he likely had his reasons," he answered, and was debating the therapy of giving her the whole damned guts of the matter when the sound of Doc's buggy rolled into the yard.

That the old man had news was obvious as soon as he came into the room. "Your deciding to give Ives Hanna another chance has paid off," he told Luke, setting down his bag and dropping his hat to haul up a chair. "Marratt, as you know, smashed both Crafkin's shoulders. Under the impression last night he wasn't long for this world, the man was persuaded by Hanna to make a complete confession. In this statement, being taken down now in front of witnesses for signing, Crafkin has admitted," Frailey told Naome, "to most of the skullduggery laid locally to your father. He has delivered himself of a terrible account in which he admits poisoning your mother and accepts full responsibility for the deaths of Jake Usher and Stanley Beckwith."

"About Dad's killing," Luke said — "did he mention why Ryerson all this time kept his mouth shut?"

"He didn't say in so many words," Frailey answered, "but the reason is plain enough from what he did say. Ryerson, so far as ranching is concerned, has always been a square peg in a round hole. Never cared about the business or been willing to assume the least interest in its details; a man of Crafkin's caliber would naturally take advantage of this. I think Ryerson must have been more than a bit uneasy now and again, but I believe we can safely assume from the record that he preferred to ignore such things as he discovered to facing the unpleasantness of putting his foot down. When at last he realized the trend events were taking Crafkin killed Jake, I'm sure, deliberately to compromise him.

"Here, according to Crafkin's statement, is what happened. The pair of them went to see Jake about acquiring this property. During the resultant conversation Jake, by Crafkin's tell of it, became extremely abusive, suddenly dropping a hand toward the butt of his pistol. Crafkin, snatching Ryerson's, fired on the instant. As Jake was falling, Crafkin, hearing the sounds of somebody coming, thrust the smoking belt gun into Ryerson's hands. You came on the scene, Luke, to see him standing with it over your father; and from that day on Crafkin has done as he pleased."

They sat quiet for awhile and presently Usher asked somewhat querulously, "When are you figurin' to let me out of this bed?"

"Isn't that woman I sent over to take care of you satisfactory?"

"I want to make a goin' concern of this spread."

"Then you'd better stay where you're at till those wounds heal. And, by the way, if Marratt should happen to drop around —"

"No danger of that. He's probably halfway to the bananas by this time."

Frailey picked up his bag. "Nevertheless, if you should happen to see him, I think you'd better tell him there's a Ranger looking this country over for him. . . ."

Marratt, after five days of living off sourdough and whatever he'd been able to knock over with a pistol, was still prowling the hills above Bella Loma, hollow-eyed, gaunt and no nearer solving his problems than he'd been the day Gainor had got his come-uppance.

The long-buried side of his nature — the part of him that cared for Naome and was willing to acknowledge this love and its indebtedness — understood Frailey and Luke

Usher were correct in believing that, for him there could be no tomorrow in the things he had found here. Better for all concerned that he get on his gray horse and either give himself up or get out of the country.

Many times after a stretch of thinking about Naome he had been in the mood to do this, but each time something had stopped him; the habit of playing God, he guessed, or the remembrance of Charlie, demanding for Ryerson the same retribution he had dumped on Hugh Clagg.

Fair was fair. Beckwith, scrambling to get his, had got a harp for his trouble. Gainor, with the example of Crafkin's steals to egg him on, had staked his whole future — and his life, as it happened — on the glimpsed possibility of breaking Wineglass and becoming top dog in the process. Their misdeeds had caught up with both of them, and with Crafkin. Did Ryerson deserve to get off scot-free with his?

Marratt's mind, sitting in judgment, rebelled against the irony of spending his life in prison for what he had done to Hugh Clagg because of Charlie while Clagg's partner, meriting a like fate, went his way untouched and unrepentant because he happened to be the father of Naome. It was too much to ask of human nature.

Marratt's mind, sitting in judgment, re-belled away with him and, crouching beside the spring where he was camped, proceeded to clean his face of whiskers. He left only the roan patch of a mustache, having generally worn one before his trouble with Clagg.

While he was hunting his pockets for the rest of the checks assembled by Naome from the reservation files he came across the badge he had taken off Hanna; and he held quiet for an interval morosely considering it. Only this bent piece of metal had stood between him-self and a hole in the ground when Crafkin's lead had hammered him into the grass of Jake's dooryard. Spared by the grace of God, some would say — but why had God both-ered? Had He saved him to settle Charlie's score against Ryerson?

Better, Marratt thought bitterly, to have croaked then and there than be faced with a future cursed with memories of a girl who could never be more to him than she had. For, no matter what course he finally took with her father, he could not ask Naome to share the fate of a brush-running fugitive. And there was nothing else in the cards for Grete Marratt but Yuma.

He cocked a look at the sky and loosed a long breath that must have come pretty near up from his bootheels. He checked over the loads in his pistol, reckoning he might just as well get about it.

He knew where to find Ryerson, had been nursing this knowledge for the past thirty hours. Before he'd turned south away from Usher's that day he had lifted a pair of high-powered binoculars from Crafkin's saddle, and with these he had kept Naome's movements under constant surveillance till he'd found the man holed-up at Straddle Bug, one of the spreads which Ryerson, through Crafkin, had taken over. No crew was being maintained there and Naome herself had ridden off about an hour ago.

He cinched the hull on the gray and thrust a boot in the stirrup. Funny he mused, how things kept coming back to you; little things, insignificant trifles which a man ought long ago to have forgotten. The weary lift of tired eyes across the length of a store porch . . . the tremulous shape of a girl's twisted smile.

Marratt, cursing, ground his teeth and slammed the horse into motion.

Raising a spurless heel above the horn of his saddle Marratt dropped to earth with eyes bleak as a gun fighter's. He loosened the weight that was sagging his shell belt and stepped onto the verandah, hollow sound rumbling out of the planks as he moved doorward — sound which fled into the hard stillness around him.

The paintless door was pulled open with a groan from dry hinges and Ryerson's face was staring into his own. The man had aged ten years since that day on the store porch. "You needn't worry," Marratt said. "I didn't come here to kill you."

The ranchman's eyes smiled tiredly. "I didn't suppose you had." He stepped back from the door. "Come in, Marratt, I've been expecting you."

Marratt looked at him suspiciously. "I imagine so," he said grimly, and raked his glance about warily as he followed the man down an uncarpeted hall.

Turning into what had evidently been the ranch office, Ryerson motioned to a chair and dropped into another behind a desk that was cluttered with papers. "You didn't hear from my daughter?"

"I've been camped in the hills ever since that fight."

"She left a couple notes at Usher's asking you to come here —"

"Did she tell you my name was Marratt?"

Ryerson nodded. "But I had already placed you. You'll remember I called you 'Luke' that day in town. I supposed you *were* Luke; as such I could understand your refusal to shake

248

and the terrible look which flashed out of your eyes when you advised me the next time we met to be armed. Riding home, however, I recalled a picture I had once come across in a Prescott paper —"

"Then you admit to having been there?"

The ranchman stared at him curiously. "Of course I've been to Prescott. As it happens, I was there just before you came to trial . . . Now you're looking," Ryerson said, voice and features expressing bewilderment, "very much as you did that day in Bella Loma —"

Marratt snarled, "How the hell did you expect me to look?"

"I don't get it," Ryerson said. "You're not Luke Usher. I don't understand why you should look as though killing me would give you a great deal of pleasure."

"Perhaps," Marratt drawled, "this will freshen up your memory," and recounted the story as he had gotten it from Charlie.

"Merciful God," Ryerson whispered when Marratt stopped speaking. "So that was the way of it . . . I don't wonder you killed him. Why didn't you tell the judge —"

"And publish her shame?"

"But to spend five years in Yuma . . ." He shook his head, swearing huskily. "And all this time you've been imagining I —"

"Do you deny it?"

"Certainly. Most vigorously. I wasn't within miles of the place when that happened."

"The girl described you."

"Of course she did —"

"And called you his partner!"

"She would have, naturally," Ryerson nodded. "We'd stopped at her place that morning to get water —"

"You and Clagg?"

"I didn't know the fellow's name. He'd ridden into my camp the night before —"

"He must have given you some kind of name."

"Yes. 'Gunderson', I believe — anyway something Scandinavian. It wasn't his right one, you may be sure of that. He showed considerable curiosity concerning the packs on my burros; since they held nothing of value I let him paw through them. I am convinced, however, that if I'd had any dust I would never have left that place alive —"

"Are you talking about Clagg?"

Ryerson showed his tired smile. "Let me finish. As I was saying, we'd stopped at this girl's place that morning for water. A couple hours after we'd left I was glad to hear him say he had decided to turn off for Skull Valley. He said, 'If I was you I wouldn't be doin' no lingerin' around here.' You may be sure I had no intention of lingering; I was too glad to be rid of him to risk a change of mind. I spent that afternoon and evening with an old friend of mine — Joe Guthrie — at his horse ranch —"

"You can prove that?"

"I imagine Joe will vouch for it. If I had thought this fellow as planning to go back to that girl's hay ranch —"

"Why don't you call him Clagg?"

"Because the man you killed wasn't Clagg, Marratt."

Marratt stared at him, speechless.

"Oh, I know," Ryerson said, "he had Clagg's badge and papers, but he was no more a marshal than you are."

Marratt eyed Naome's father an uncomfortable while, at last asking, "What kind of a shine are you trying to cut?" He got his wind back then and said, suddenly furious: "Maybe you've forgotten I was tried, convicted and sentenced to Yuma for killing Hugh Clagg, a deputy U.S. marshal!"

"I *had* forgotten it until I learned the other day of your escape. But I know Clagg, and the fellow who went with me to that girl's place after water was not Clagg —"

"How long have you known this?"

Ryerson shrugged and said tiredly, "The man didn't try to pass himself off as Clagg to

251

me, remember. He gave me to understand he was some kind of agent for the Federal Narcotics Bureau. It wasn't until I saw his picture with yours in that Prescott paper that I realized the supposed Clagg I'd been hearing about was this Gunderson. Joe Guthrie had sent me this paper at the ranch and it was six months old when I came back from a trip and read it.

"I meant to do something about it but someway or another I became busy with other matters and it completely slipped my mind. You had refused to make any statement at the time of your arrest. Even had I been in the habit of keeping abreast of current events I would have had no reason to connect this man's killing with the girl at whose shack we had stopped that morning for water."

Ryerson sighed. "Since the death of my wife I've been little concerned with the things going on in the world of the present. Too little concerned, a lot of people would say. My coming onto you that day in Bella Loma was quite a shock, particularly when I realized you were Marratt and not Luke Usher. I'm deeding back to their original owners the various properties taken over in my name by Crafkin. I've sent Frailey, for young Usher, a substantial check for the fifteen years I've been told Jake's grass fed my cattle, and another for the stock Naome tells me Crafkin stole.

"I'm not trying to put myself in a better light with anyone; I'm simply trying as best I can to make what amends are possible. After bumping into you with Frailey and my daughter on the porch of Danvers' store, I came home and dug up that paper. I enclosed it with an exhaustive letter of true particulars which I sent posthaste to the Governor. His answer came yesterday."

Ryerson picked up an official envelope which he pushed across the desk toward Marratt who, with no move to touch it, said through the whirl of his churning thoughts, "You've thrown over any chance you ever had of going to Phoenix."

The ranchman smiled his tired smile. "I never wanted to be governor. There again I followed the path of least resistance, letting another man's persuasion urge me into making a not very praiseworthy effort. I told the — But why don't you read that letter?"

Marratt shook his head. "I wouldn't know straight-up from down, right now —"

"Then I must tell you that an investigation, based on the facts revealed in my letter, has proved my contention. The man you killed was not Clagg but a notorious outlaw for whom —"

"I think," declared a voice from the open

door back of Marratt, "that what this fellow will most enjoy hearing now is that, to all intents and purposes, he's no longer a fugitive from justice."

Marratt, twisting his head, could only gawk at him stupidly.

"That's right," said Ranger Smith, grinning pleasantly. "I've been instructed to give you notice you'll be expected in the Governor's office on the seventeenth for questioning at one o'clock sharp. You may be held up a week or two, but I guess I can safely prophesy that, once all the official red tape's been unwound, you'll be free as a bird."

"Free!" Marratt said and, then, to Ryerson: "Where's Naome?"

W